The Disaster Relief Club
An O Line Mystery

M. Saylor Billings

Billibatt Productions

The Disaster Relief Club

M. Saylor Billings

The Disaster Relief Club - An O Line Mystery

Copyright © 2011 by M. Saylor Billings

Library of Congress Catalog Card Number: 2011961641
ISBN: 978-09838061-3-4
Billibatt Productions
http://www.billibatt.com
olinemysteries@gmail.com

The Disaster Relief Club

DEDICATION:

For all those who survive adversity,

and can still find laughter in their hearts.

The Disaster Relief Club

M. Saylor Billings

TABLE OF CONTENTS

Acknowledgments

Prologue   1

1   Did ya' feel it?   11

2   Allies   27

3   Old sins have long shadows   41

4   Dert Bags   59

5   Search and Rescue   75

6   The Women's Golf Club   91

7   Chinese Walls   109

8   Circles Don't have Sides   127

9   Every Pot's Lid   147

10 Sally's New Friend   167

11 Tim and Michael Alliance   187

12 Dragons VS. Dert Bags   205

Epilogue   225

The Disaster Relief Club

ACKNOWLEDGMENTS

For her help with this book the author is
particularly grateful to Raejean M. Battin,
otherwise known as "Reader of a thousand drafts".

PROLOGUE

Jimmy Marsh's eyes stared up from the oil-changing pit. His mouth still bore the mirth he had felt just before his brainstem fractured at the spinal column. Warm blood oozed down his back onto the cold cement. Tucked into his pants, stuffed haphazardly under his shirt, was a thick manila envelope with the Dragon Emergency Management logo stamped on it.

Urgent streaks of yellow and white headlamps pierced the pitch black above his body. The approaching muffled thumps of steel-toed boots echoed through the abandoned airplane hangar. Commander Bill White used his flashlight to survey the damage to his makeshift command post, which consisted of a foldable card table, a foldable chair, a battery operated lantern, and a cardboard box that contained his paperwork.

Commander Bill White picked up the lantern, snapped it on, and snarled at the two smiling faces approaching him.

"Did ya' feel *that*?" Wyatt boomed, his youthful energy ricocheting around the abandoned military base hangar.

"So much for the drill, that's the real thing!" Charley added, watching the dust dance around in the light beams.

"Shut up – both of you. Go back to your stations and start packing up. We have to get out of here. You've got 10 minutes." Bill said in his Oklahoma drawl.

"My men are on it, Chief." Charley said.

"Yeah, you can hear it coming like thunder rumblings, but below you." Wyatt explained.

"If either one of you leave one scrap of evidence that we were here, I *will* kill you." Bill's thin lips trembled.

Wyatt tapped on Charley's arm and pulled him backwards, "Back in ten Commander."

Commander Bill righted the desk up and placed the lantern on top. The contents of his box – area maps, payroll sheets, forms and documents – had all spilled out across the floor. He shook his head in frustration. The one and only night he could be sure there would be no outside interference to run a mock earthquake drill inside his target area and there is an *actual* earthquake. He paced along the shadowy boundary of his lantern light and kicked an orange pylon that had scooted inside his outline into the oil-changing pit beyond. Muffled boots approached.

"Commander, I have my men packing up the last of the our radio equipment. We'll be ready to roll out in five minutes. Should I just have them all meet back at the off-site base?" Austin looked over his shoulder as Greg approached from behind him.

"Yeah, let's just all go – no. You take your men and equipment through the Warner tunnel, medical and haz-mat should take the South Bridge. And have flight office, incident command, and utility go with me around Oakland. We'll do a quick debriefing and then breakfast – I rented out the back room at Sunshine's."

"We're ready now Sir," Greg addressed the Commander and then turned to Austin. "Austin, I sent a couple of my men over to help pull that tent down for you," Greg began.

Austin ignored Greg. "Sir, I know we'll be doing a debriefing but you should know there was some interference on the radio's before we went silent."

Commander Bill squared his small shoulders to Austin, the lantern highlighting half his face. "What are you going to do about that Austin?"

"Run equipment tests, come back out here to the base, maybe, and do some run —throughs at night again."

"Yeah, ya' think? Maybe?" Bill shook his head, making the excess skin on his neck waggle. "Keep drilling. There will be no mistakes or *hiccups* in our outfit. Understand?"

"Sir, I do." Austin turned, leaving Greg facing Commander Bill.

"What do you want, ass wipe." It was a command not a question.

"I came to help you pack up Sir."

"*I* don't need *your* help. No one leaves before meeting back here and you can lead them in prayer before the exit."

"Sir. Yes sir."

Wyatt switched on his headlamp and looked around at the five men hanging around the white medical van. "Prayer with Commander before we leave. Hop to it." He said.

Groans and mumbling accompanied the moving bodies. Wyatt pulled Charley aside. "I'm beginning to think Jimmy may have been the lucky one."

"I don't think anyone who knows Jimmy would call him lucky."

Wyatt struck a serious tone with his childhood friend, "Look, after tonight, I'm just not sure this is the right place for either of us."

"You're just mad they made you cut your hair." Charley said as he pointed at Wyatt's fresh 'high and tight' haircut.

"Charley, listen to me, man. Maybe Jimmy was right about this job."

Charley stopped his friend, "That's easy for you to say *Wyatt*. But for Jimmy and me, it's different. We're nurses. Where else are we going to make these kinds of bones? Look if you want to leave, then go."

"No, but let's hear Jimmy out. He's over at Stranglers – we'll talk to him. I don't think he's mad because he didn't get hired..." Wyatt's volume was growing.

Charley grabbed Wyatt's arm sharply. "Shh. Fine, just keep your voice down and walk – I don't want to be late for the prayer thing."

Agnes Strangler rocked her eighty-three year old body up and out of bed at 4:07 a.m. "Oh, that was a good one." She put on her housecoat and matching slippers. Reaching below her bed, she pulled out her oversized suede "fashion" bag that she had converted into her evacuation kit and drug it behind her as she opened her bedroom door and entered the hall.

"Jimmy?" She knocked on a bedroom door. Agnes Strangler's best friend had been Ruth Marsh, Jimmy's grandmother. Before Ruth died, Agnes promised to help look after Jimmy. Now Jimmy was staying in Agnes's guest room while he looked for a job and together the two were enrolled in Ohlone Island's Disaster Emergency Response Teams, or DERT, program. Both Agnes and Ruth often thought of Jimmy as a strange boy. He wasn't really 'serial killer' strange – as a matter of fact, he just didn't have any kind of killer instincts in him.

And for two women of *the greatest generation*, that was strange. Despite his Grandma Ruth's best efforts to but some vim and vigor in him, Jimmy had remained passive. But Agnes had taken up the mantle through card games. And she believed Jimmy was actually starting to come around. Even last night she thought she heard him go out very late. Perhaps he's even found a girl? Agnes thought Ruth would be so excited.

"Jimmy?" Agnes opened the bedroom door a bit and then wider to reveal an empty room. The bed had been made up and Jimmy's overnight bag sat at the foot of the bed.

"Huh." Agnes said aloud. What is it Jimmy and his friends say? What was that phrase she heard? Jiggy? No, hooty, a hooty call – that was it. Maybe Jimmy was on a hooty call. She pulled the door shut again and continued padding around the house dragging her evacuation purse with her. After she did a cursory walk through and picked up a few fallen items, she returned back to her bedroom and slipped her purse back under the bed.

Just as she began to dose off again, the doorbell rang. Maybe it was Jimmy, she thought snickering - caught out on his hooty call by an earthquake. But the vigorous knocking made her change her mind, and she could hear Roseanne Featherstone's nasally voice calling out, "Ms. Strangler!" "Ms. Strangler!"

"Can you see anything, Running Bear?" Roseanne asked her husband Ronald "Running Bear" Featherstone.

He moved over to the side of the stoop, cupping his hands and peering into the picture window. "No, knock again."

Agnes slid her feet into her slippers again and flung her robe around herself. "Now these two idiots," she mumbled. Agnes did not like Ronald "Running Bear" or

Roseanne Featherstone. They were of the 1960's San Francisco counterculture, those who had dropped out, but unlike Ben and Jerry, they never tuned back in. The Featherstone's had been in her Red Cross first aid class and were continuing on in the DERT program as well. So now these two idiots are brain surgeons, she thought, padding to the front door.

Agnes threw open the front door. The porch light gleamed off Ronald's bald spot in the center of his pageboy haircut. If Sonny and Cher had aged naturally but never changed their stage outfits – Agnes curled her upper lip at them in a grin.

"Are you okay?" Ronald asked Agnes.

Agnes pointed at him, "What is that?"

Ronald shrugged the rug on his back. "It's my buffalo hide."

"That's disgusting." She looked at Roseanne. "That's your first responder outfit?" Roseanne was wearing a layered chiffon robe and corked high heals.

"We just came by to see that you were all right," Roseanne offered.

"Of course I am. I don't live in a teepee."

"Neither do we Mrs. Strangler," Ronald offered. "Is Jimmy here with you?"

"Jimmy's asleep, like I should be. Good bye." Ms. Strangler shut the door on the Featherstone's and turned back for the bedroom.

What bothered Agnes the most about the Featherstone's was their growing interest in Jimmy. If they were looking for someone to buy their drugs, then they were looking in the wrong direction with her Jimmy.

Wyatt and Charley sat in the derelict trailer office of Commander Bill White. Commander Bill stared at the two of them for a moment from behind his desk. Charley was feeling the weight of the all-nighter coupled with a large breakfast. His eyelids were heavy, and he was drooping slightly. Wyatt on the other hand was more alert, or perhaps, alarmed. Bill White did not like these two young men who sat before him and made no pretense of it now. His main goal since he had met these two California Pansies was to get rid of them as fast as possible.

The Federal Disaster Management Agency, FDMA, was about to start farming out disaster response work to private companies. Bill White's bosses at Dragon Logistics wanted to be the highest bidders. This specific contract was strategically very important for the West Coast operations of Dragon Logistics' emergency management division. The Island City of Ohlone sits in the San Francisco Bay and still holds the structural bones of the decommissioned airfield on a closed military base at the north end of the island. Having control over this area and its airspace through a federal contract meant Dragon Logistics would have security and emergency control over all of Northern California and a large financial slice of the security and disaster services pie.

The Commander's job was to set up and to train the tactical emergency response teams for Dragon Logistics. Why the home office would not allow him to assemble his own teams on such an important assignment was beyond him. Unfortunately Bill had been saddled with the San Francisco Bay Area, an area famous for its non-conformists. But there was always a way around orders from the Maryland home office and by chance Bill's way just fell into his own lap.

"I've been keeping a close eye on you two..."

Charley held his breath. Suddenly he was not as sleepy as he thought.

Commander Bill continued, "... and I was asked by the home office to offer up my brightest men for a special assignment. There's a pay raise in it, which is why I didn't have you fill out your pay forms earlier."

Charley let out his breath in an audible sigh catching the Commander and Wyatt's attention. "Pardon me, Sir."

"Have you heard of DERT?"

Both men instinctively lied in unison shaking their heads no.

"DERT, Disaster Emergency Response Teams. They're neighborhood watch teams but for disaster emergencies. Very disorganized, very untrained, and frankly very dangerous. The problem is FDMA, in all its wisdom, has granted local municipalities money to organize these groups in hopes of saving lives." The Commander let out a choked chuckle. "The problem is now we have two chefs in the kitchen. See?"

Both men nodded.

"And we can't have two chefs in the kitchen. So I've been asked to send two of my brightest into the DERT program and report their training and their tactical arrangements to my superiors."

Both men nodded.

"Good. Now you'll be starting late into the program but I imagine with your abilities you'll catch right up to them. I believe the first class starts tomorrow evening so I'll expect full written reports the following Monday. That's all. Oh, wait, here's your new paperwork for the assignment. Fill it out and just return it on Monday with your reports."

Wyatt stood up first. "Thank you Commander."

Charley followed Wyatt quickly. "Sir."

The Commander watched the men leave through his trailer window. The taller one, Charley, tried to high five his friend who was walking with his head down.

"Dude, we just got a raise. I thought he hated me and I know he hated you. He hated your hair, dude." Charley was ebullient.

"Just get to the car Charley. Put your hand down. Can't you see what just happened?" Wyatt made his way to the driver's side of his Jeep and got in.

"What? We just got a raise and no more of *Wild Bill Hiccup*! It's awesome!"

Wyatt didn't respond yet. He drove off quickly out of Commander Bill's sight.

"Charley, we just got fired," Wyatt explained.

"We just got a special assignment. What are you talking about?"

"Dude, listen, we were not hired by Commander Bill. We were hired through a recruiter from Dragon Logistics' home office. Now, Commander Bill has had enough time here to figure out who he wants on his team, and we're not those people. So he can't exactly fire us, instead he just takes us off the scene. It would be like putting a dermatology nurse in the E.C.U. – you understand?"

"But that can be done, with the right training," Charley countered.

"Ah. See with the *right training*. Aren't we a little over trained for a neighborhood watch now?"

"Well what the shit do we do? I can't just quit."

"Do what you want. I'm going home and putting my resume back together."

"Dude, you can't quit," Charley pleaded.

"No, but I can put out some job feelers while I'm putting up with this bullshit. Charley, I'm sorry, but the writing is on the wall, man."

The Disaster Relief Club

CHAPTER 1

DID YA' FEEL IT?

Lorna Tollison rocked gently with the swaying earth and sighed awake. She lulled over onto her back and opened her sleepy eyes just in time to see her partner, Sally Thompson, hovering mid-air just above her head. Sally came crashing down with a thud, muffling Lorna's scream. The bed fell off its rail, tumbling them both onto the floor.

"Have you lost your fucking mind?" Lorna cried out.

"You didn't wake up!" Sally said. "I was in the doorway."

"What?"

"There was an earthquake and you didn't wake up. I had to come back from the doorway to cover you."

"Ah, you were protecting me. Now get off. You're crushing me."

"I'm sorry." Sally rolled the rest of the way off the mattress as Lorna struggled to untangle herself from the sheets.

"I can't believe I didn't wake up. What do we do now? I mean is there going to be another one, like an aftershock?"

Sally pulled on her robe. "I don't know. We better turn on the news."

The living room looked like it had been ransacked. Books and videos had fallen off the shelves and a lamp leaned precariously on the table. Fortitude, one of their blonde tabbies, came out of Lorna's office meowing loudly.

"Where's Patience?" Sally asked looking around.

"I know where he is." Lorna announced walking into her office and lifting an old airline blanket from a basket. Patience looked up at her and meowed before leaping into her arms. "It's okay, momma's baby. Sshh. I got you."

Sally rolled her eyes as she turned back into the living room and clicked on the television.

Lorna walked around the rented Victorian home accessing the damage with Patience mewing in her arms. They had moved from New York City and lived in this old Victorian home for a couple of years now but this was Lorna's first earthquake experience. Lorna could hear the upstairs neighbors milling about as she crossed into the kitchen. The quake had opened some of the cabinets and spilled out their contents onto the counter and floor, but hadn't broken anything. No glass shards at least. Lorna cocked her head to the side and looked at the sink that sat on the far outside wall, then rolled her head to the other side. She focused on the cabinets again and ran her eyes along the bottom. Were they always slanted like that?

"Where's the flashlight?" Sally popped her head into the kitchen.

Lorna shrugged. "Come here. Are we sinking?"

Sally leaned to the side. "Oh. Yeah. Well, that's not good."

"There's one on my key ring."

"I know but don't we have a big one? I want to check the car. Make sure that carport is still standing."

"There might be one in the foyer cabinet, with the candles."

Sally left Lorna staring at the kitchen sink. What if this had been a bad earthquake? Where would they go if half the house fell in? Patience jumped out of her arms onto the floor and let himself out the cat door.

"Four point eight by the way," Sally said as she came back through the kitchen following the cat into the backyard.

Lorna looked at the clock. 4:15. What would have happened if Sally hadn't thought to come back for her? How could I let myself be caught off guard? Why am I standing here like a melting popsicle, letting Sally do all the work? Am I in shock?

Lorna and Sally had survived the September 11th attacks in New York City. Although they hadn't known each other at the time, both had been going to their respective offices, each a couple of blocks away from the World Trade Center that morning. And both had returned home to their respective apartments covered in white dust. A few hours after the buildings collapsed, Lorna had pulled herself together, showered, and thrown her laptop and few items in a backpack to make her escape from the city. Perez, her adopted older sister's chauffeur and handy man, met her at her apartment door. A short man of Spanish European and Mayan decent, Perez was dressed in military fatigues, a leather bomber jacket, and a white scarf.

13

"I come to rescue Meeez. Lorna. Come with me."

Lorna towered over him by four inches. "No. This is wrong. I'm staying. I'm a journalist. It's what I do. Look at me Perez – I'm fine. Go back and tell my dad and Tessa I'm okay."

Perez hadn't moved. He looked up at her defiantly, "No. Today jew are my sharsh, come with me."

"I'm your what?"

"My sharsh. Get jew bag."

"What's a sharsh."

"Sharsh, sharsh. My credit *sharsh*."

"I'm your credit card?" Lorna knew exactly what Perez meant but stalled for time. "Perez, how did you even get here?"

As Perez grew more frustrated his dialect became thicker. "No. No fooling. Jew'er no shanging the subject on me. Rojo said to knock jew out, eef I had too. And jewer Papa said jez too. I am to knock jew on da head and carry jew eef I have to all the way to H-Atlantah."

"Rojo" was Perez's nickname for Tessa, due to her trademark wild curly red hair.

Despite being blind Tessa was a successful computer engineer who had invented, with her adopted father's help, several voice-command computer aide devises for the blind. Her father then repurposed many of the devices for the use in security and secret services by the government. As a result, Tessa was an industry unto herself. Tessa was, if nothing else, a very determined woman.

Lorna looked down at his stubby index finger pointing up to her, and out the window at the dark plume in the sky, and gave up the battle. "Let me get a few more things. I want to be back here in two days, Perez!"

"Eef it is still here *I* will bring jew back myself."

A boat ride, a motorcycle ride, a helicopter ride and a long car drive later, Lorna sat in her father's kitchen with Tessa and Perez watching the television coverage.

Sally came back in and stared at Lorna for a moment. Lorna hadn't moved. She was still staring at the bottom of the cabinets in the kitchen.

"Honey?"

No, Lorna thought, this won't do. I'm a go-getter. I'm proactive. This is not who I am. I am not a sitting duck. No one has to *rescue* me. I'm a survivor, *with moxie*! Lorna turned on Sally. "Where were you?"

"I was in the garage. Are you okay?"

"Of course I am. Get the boys. We have to get ready."

"For what?"

"I don't know."

"Lorna, honey, go sit down for a minute. I'll fix us some breakfast."

"No, I'll fix the breakfast. You go sit down."

Sally paused and looked around. "Did something happen?"

"Just an *earthquake*. And what was I doing? Nothing. I was sleeping."

"You're a heavy sleeper."

"Sally, I *slept* through an *earthquake*."

"It was a light earthquake. Come on, let's have a big breakfast and we'll talk about it. Maybe I overacted. I shouldn't have flown at you like that. What a horrible way to wake up." Sally reached out for Lorna to embrace her.

A knock at the door interrupted them. Sally looked at the stove clock before opening the front door to their friend Tim.

"You guys alright?" Tim smiled.

Lorna popped out from behind Sally, "Of course we are –" but stopped herself when she got a good look at Tim. He wore a yellow reflector vest and a yellow safety helmet and a bright yellow backpack. "What are you wearing?"

"I'm a DERT member. I have a badge."

Sally caught her laugh in her throat and choked a little. "Come in Tim. I was just about to make some coffee."

"Thanks, I can't. I need to check the rest of the houses on this street."

Lorna reached a long arm out of the doorway and grabbed Tim by the vest. "They're fine. Get in here. Where's Annie?"

Annie, Tim's wife, was Lorna's best friend on Ohlone Island. They had met when Lorna had gotten lost on her first trip to San Francisco and wound up on Ohlone Island instead. As it turned out, Lorna had rented the apartment in the Victorian house that sat catty-corner to Tim and Annie's house. As both women worked from home, they became fast friends.

"She's asleep."

"She slept through it too?" Lorna was delighted.

"No, she went back to bed after we calmed the dogs."

"Oh," Lorna nodded in disappointment. "So what is this dirt thing?"

"It's Disaster Emergency Response Teams, or just DERT. It's organized through the fire department and sectioned off by neighborhoods. We're in the 8th section."

"Ha!" Lorna cried out momentarily. "Sorry."

Tim stared at her blankly.

Lorna explained her outburst. "Section 8? Mentally unfit for duty?"

"Oh, no. It's the area section number."

"So, okay, how does this work? What's in your backpack there?"

"You sign up for the classes and then you do training. Anyone can join. Kids, the elderly, special needs, even you can join." Tim pulled off his backpack. "This is my response pack. Flashlights, crowbar, water, first aid – stuff like that."

Lorna was keenly interested in his presentation and continued listening.

Tim paused before continuing. "It helps regular people who are generally first on the scene, you know, in disasters, learn what to do and what not to do. We have drills all the time down at the old base. And you can join whatever division you feel comfortable with. Like, there's a ham radio section or a medical or haz-mat. It's a way for people to help themselves in their communities instead of relying on the fire department who can't be everywhere in a disaster. It's really helped me learn to think on my feet."

Lorna had heard enough. A weight had been lifted off her shoulders. There was a way to help herself, a place to go to learn what to do in these types of situations. She repeated the line to Tim, nodding, "learn to think on my feet." She didn't have to stand there like a melting popsicle – she would know what to do. She grabbed Tim's arm gently, "Tim, I want to be DERT. Can you get me into the DERT?"

A tear ran down Lorna's cheek as Sally walked back in with a coffee tray, "Oh God, what happened?"

Tim smiled at Sally. "Lorna's joining DERT and Annie's going with her."

Lorna perked up. "She is?"

"Yes, she absolutely is. How about you Sally?"

Sally almost dropped the coffee tray and rushed over to the coffee table to put it down.

But Lorna jumped in, "Sally's a runner, right, Sally?"

"Yes, I tend to get out of harm's way."

"She left me in the bed to be crushed just now."

"I did. Before I went back for her."

"And you already had aid training, when you went to Bosnia, didn't you?"

Tim suddenly stopped repacking his response kit. "You were in Bosnia?"

Sally tensed up. "Briefly. Aid work. It was my Grandmother's idea of an extra curricular activity to get into law school." Sally shook her head. She wanted this conversation to end. "It was a bad experience and I don't like to talk about it."

Tim continued, "Yeah, but you were in 9-11 and did relief work in *Bosnia*? You'd be perfect for DERT."

"No Tim, those experiences taught be that I'm not perfect for DERT." Sally was done with this conversation.

"You must have been very young."

"I was and impressionable. So, coffee or do you need to continue on your rounds?" Sally was already walking to the front door as she asked the question.

"I should go, make sure the block is at least structurally sound, nobody's fallen and can't get up," Tim said, taking Sally's cue.

"Wait, what do I do now?" Lorna asked.

"Go online for the DERT program for Ohlone Island. I think it's DERT dot o-r-g and then put in your zip code. They have classes almost every week. FDMA gave them a bunch of money so they're coupling up with the Red Cross. Start there."

This caught Sally's attention. "A federal agency is giving money to the Red Cross?"

"Yeah, see, the government mandates the Red Cross to exist but doesn't provide them with funds, so I guess this coupling is just kind of a work around for some federal funds. Whatever, y'know, it all helps," Tim shrugged.

Lorna bounced up and walked Tim to the door. "Thank you Tim."

Tim gave a sheepish grin. "You're welcome." He heaved the backpack over his shoulder and said cheerfully, "All in a day's work!"

Lorna was brimming with excitement as she shut the door behind him and turned to face Sally. "It's like manna from the heavens. I recognize a need, I decide to take action, and the universe meets me half way."

"Good. And you have a buddy to go with you. Breakfast?"

"Yeah, but first, I know we've talked about this before but I feel like I did all the talking." Lorna followed Sally into the kitchen. "What happened to you *that day*?"

Sally did not need to know which day Lorna was referring to. Like thousands of survivors of the September 11th attacks, *that day* is always referred to as "that day". Sally pulled out some eggs from the refrigerator. "Nothing, really. I mean our office was a couple of blocks from the World Trade Center and we were evacuated just before the second tower fell. It was utter chaos. So I ran. I ran all the way across the Brooklyn Bridge and walked for about an hour and a half back home. I got home, took a long hot shower and got whatever that, dust or ash, was off, poured a Scotch and turned on the television. And sat there for a week until they called and said come back to work. So I did."

"That's it? You never processed it with anyone?"

"What do you mean?"

"Like a therapist maybe?"

"No. I mean we talked about it a lot at work. They brought in a social worker or psychologist, whatever, for people who were *really* having a hard time with it. There was a lot of grieving and y'know funerals we went to. But no, there was no formal... uh..." Sally paused in breaking the eggs and looked up "...like debriefing. No."

They smiled awkwardly at each other for a moment.

"Oh." Lorna got up from the kitchen table as the phone rang. She loved Sally unconditionally, but honestly, sometimes Sally felt as foreign to her as a stranger. "That'll be Tessa. I'll get it."

Sally closed her eyes and took a deep breath – in through the nose and out through her mouth, as the psychologist had taught her. The Bosnia aid story she had told to Tim and Lorna was true, for the most part. Her Grandmother *had* convinced her to go to Bosnia but it was under the *guise* of aid work. It was a story she stuck to so much she almost believed it herself.

But in truth, Sally's Grandfather had been in the CIA – in the beginning when it was formed and became something of a war hero, not that anyone outside the CIA would ever know it. Her parents kept up this family tradition and followed in his footprints as covert agents within American Embassies around the world. Sally's mother is of Chinese heritage and her father is Portuguese/English so Sally, in contrast, has an Eastern European look about her. No doubt Grandma Soucek had this in mind when she offered Sally up as next in line to the CIA for training. Sally had been raised by her Grandma Soucek to believe that her parents were embassy workers in foreign countries because they spoke so many foreign languages. And Sally really believed she was going to the Bosnian region as a foreign aid worker to help the people recover from the horrible war and genocide they had endured. Grandma Soucek had pulled strings and convinced the CIA to fast track her granddaughter, in light of the family tradition, and sent a very naïve Sally into the heart of a war without any formal training and without giving Sally any say as to her own future. In hindsight, it was an absolutely unconscionable thing to do in Sally's mind.

Sally was slow to pick up what exactly she had been really doing there. It had made sense to her that her trainers gave her a gun and taught her to use it for her own protection, because unlike many of her fellow aid workers, Sally actually did look like she could have been from the region. She began as a runner. Running errands from one camp to the next, making stops along the way.

But the language her trainers used was changing – errands became missions. Sally had not put together the actual word "intel" with what she had been doing, until she heard a trainer use the term off handedly.

Then reality came scorching down on her one night when she had been paired with a nurse from the medical group to do a "drop". A word her parents had used during a visit when they were relating an embassy work story to her Grandma Soucek. Sally was being told how dangerous this *drop* might be and did she feel comfortable with the gun.

It will be a last measure of course, but all the same. Don't worry – everyone has to go through it. The Nurse will be with you and she knows the ropes.

At that moment Sally wanted to run. All those years she believed her absentee parents to be Embassy workers – did she ever think to ask doing what? She assumed it meant that they translated documents, or ran the janitorial staff, processed passports or helped out wayward American tourists, things like that. It had all been a lie.

When Sally returned to the States, she promptly entered law school, never mentioning the Bosnia situation again. The CIA pursued her, as she expected, but she always politely declined. She cut her ties with the people with whom she had worked in Bosnia and kept her Grandma Soucek at arm's length.

In 1999, her parents retired from "the service" by faking their own deaths. Sally saw an opportunity and changed her name and changed her job in hopes of putting as much distance between herself and her past as she could. The CIA had long since stopped trying to recruit Sally even after the September 11th attacks when she hid in her apartment shaken to her core by that day's events. Only in the last couple of years she realized that perhaps her past was beginning to catch up with her. And she didn't like it. She wanted to run again.

"So Tessa has an idea."

Sally put the orange juice bottle down sat at the kitchen table with Lorna. "Tessa *is* an idea."

"She wants to put together emergency kits for the blind and infirmed."

"As a business venture?"

"No, as a charity."

"Well, I mean you'd have to get pretty specific, according to the, uh.. specific capabilities." Sally shook her head.

"You mean disabilities."

"Hey, I used that word one time in front of your family and almost had my head handed to me. So no, I mean *capabilities*."

Lorna giggled, "Yeah, Tessa can be kinda militant about those things."

Sally lifted her eyebrows at Lorna.

Lorna nodded back at her agreeing, "I hear ya. Anyway, she said she had a break in her schedule coming up and was thinking about coming for a visit. What do you think of that?"

"Great. When's she coming?"

"I don't know. I'd guess in a few weeks?"

"That's fine. Should I put in for a couple of days off?"

"If you can, maybe. But ya' know, don't cut yourself short on Tessa's account."

"No, I've got some use or lose time accrued so it's fine. Just let me know when."

"Okay," Lorna mumbled over a mouthful of toast and jam.

Sally had worked as an attorney for the Federal Department of Housing and Urban Development, or

HUD for short, since 1999. In those eight years, she had taken only four sick days.

Sally glanced at the clock. 5:30. "I'm just going to shower and go in I think. What are you doing today?"

"Well," Lorna started. "First I have to fix the bed."

"Oh, I'll help you with that before I go."

"Good, then I'm going to take a nap. Then I need to finish that article for publication and I'm signing up for the DERT classes and reading some material about—"

The house shook beneath them suddenly and Sally snapped up her orange juice glass as Lorna held on to the kitchen table.

"DUDE!" Lorna cried out.

Sally grabbed Lorna's hand. "It's just an aftershock, it's okay."

"You know we're going to have to move now."

"What? Why?"

"Look at this kitchen – it's leaning. And the in living room, in the front, that's leaning too. There's a crack where the window sill meets the window."

"Sweetheart, this house stood through the 1906 quake and the Loma Prieta in 89 and it was retrofitted, I don't think a small tumbler is going to take it down."

"You don't *know* that. May I remind you about the straw that breaks the camel's back?"

Sally could see she would not win this one no matter what and quickly changed her tactics.

"Okay, that's true. Who really knows what could happen?" She took another bite of eggs. "Do you want the rest of the eggs?"

Lorna's eyes jutted about nervously. "No, I have *things* to do."

Sally saw the distress in Lorna's eyes and scooted her chair around to face Lorna. "Come here. Listen to me." Lorna swiveled her chair around to face Sally.

"Are you going to talk to me like a child?"

"No. But I am going to try to reason with you. I think I know what you are feeling."

"I'm scared as shit dude!"

"Yes, not knowing when the earth is going to open up and swallow hard is unnerving if you dwell on it. So I'm glad you are going to take the DERT class. At least one of us will know what to do. But," Sally took a deep breath, "over the past year or so I've noticed a change in your work habits."

Lorna bristled. "What do you mean?"

"I mean, when we were in New York you were doing two and three articles a week and then restructuring them under various pseudonyms and sending them out to three or four different publications. You were busy, busy, busy all the time."

"There's not a lot happening on an island in the middle of the San Francisco Bay, Sally. This place isn't exactly world renowned for its couture and museums and whatever."

"No, it's not. Which is why I was thinking maybe it's time you really start writing some longer – what do you call it – long form fiction, or non-fiction. Maybe take another stab at your satire book you were always going on about."

"Nobody, really, likes you."

"Right."

Lorna sighed. "Where is this coming from?"

"It's just that I've noticed, I mean, I think you're getting bored with the articles. Maybe? A little?"

"Yeah. But it's my job. It's what I do."

"Doesn't mean you have to do it forever. Where's the rule that says Lorna Tollison, or Rebecca Charles, or Robert Cook – that Drugstore Publishing only does magazine articles. I'm just saying maybe branch out a little?"

"But I keep busy. Are you saying I need to pull in more money? Is that what this is about?"

"No." Sally continued, "Lorna, you are always getting distracted always getting involved with that Detective Keeling on some weird island thing. Had this happened in New York, you'd be out on the street interviewing people for an article by now, not worrying about a leaning kitchen. You need a change."

Lorna shook her head.

Sally shook her head back, smiling. "Take the chance, honey."

"I'll think about it." Lorna got up and put her plate in the sink. "But don't think *you* are distracting *me* from what just happened."

"Damn, I just played my last ace too." Sally followed Lorna to the sink. "Look I do have a small emergency kit. Something to get us started."

"You do?"

"Of course, I put it away when we moved here to earthquake country."

"Where is it?" Lorna asked.

Sally walked into the bedroom and came back promptly with a wad of cash and held it out.

Lorna looked at it. "*That's* our emergency kit?"

"Yes."

Lorna blinked at her partner. "You are *so* weird."

Sally shuffled off several large bills. "Here. We'll probably need some water too. Or something."

Lorna shook her head and smiled. "Thank you," she said and kissed Sally.

The Disaster Relief Club

CHAPTER 2

ALLIES

Michael pulled himself up the rocky estuary embankment and paused there for a moment. He had to catch his breath, just for a minute. The ringing in his ears amplified the throbbing pain in his leg. Two arms reached down and pulled him further up the embankment and rolled him over. He opened his eyes to see a pair of police issue shiny shoes near his head.

"Come on, just a little further." The voice sounded muffled under the ringing.

Michael looked up to the voice. "Just give me a minute."

From the firelight glowing across the estuary, he could see a man in dark clothing, a running jacket maybe. The sailboat he had been on when it blew up, its neighboring boat, and the dock were still on fire. But the shoes, those are cop shoes.

"Now. You looked like a beached whale out here." The voice was close to his ear, sounding soft and clear.

Michael recognized the code signal but his brain couldn't come up with a counter sign. "I don't understand your shoes." It was the truth and all he could come up with.

"You're not hurt. Come on, you can walk five steps. I'll help you." The man helped Michael to his feet and shuffled him to the squad car. But it was twenty steps – Michael had counted them, before he was laid carefully across the plastic back seat.

"Hang on now. We're going to get help." The man's voice was concerned as he took his jacket off and placed it over Michael and shut the door.

I have to get out of here, Michael thought. Time seemed to lurch ahead and stand still. He could hear the man's muffled voice coming from the front seat. He was talking to someone else. He was on a phone maybe. Time lurched ahead again and the car came to a stop. Someone else got in the front seat and they were moving again. Michael opened his eyes briefly to see a dark figure. He opened them again and he was being moved and there was talking.

Sergeant Roberta Fitzgerald looked down at Michael's body as he stirred. He looked like a giant in that child's bed. Michael opened his eyes to see a black woman in a police uniform staring at him. She looked away and Michael followed her gaze to a white man in a running suit who was leaning against a little clothing dresser. The walls had red clowns and balloons attached to them. They watched Michael struggle awake. Michael took several deep breathes before speaking.

"Where am I?"

"My kid's bed." Detective Keeling said.

"Who are you?"

"I'm Detective Keeling and this is Sergeant Fitzgerald of the Ohlone Police Department." Keeling looked at his watch. "It's almost three a.m. Okay. Do you know who blew up those boats?"

"No."

"Do you know Schwartz? Was he on the boat?"

"Who?"

"Don't fuck with me, kid."

"No, I don't know what his name was. The old man, he was there."

Michael struggled to sit up. His head felt so heavy. Everything hurt. He lifted the sheet and gazed down at his naked body to his bandaged leg. He looked at Sergeant Fitzgerald mumbled accusingly, "Where are my clothes?"

Fitzgerald chuckled, "I'm having them pressed for you. What's your name?"

Michael leaned his head back down, "Michael."

"Okay, Michael. Here's what we know. You arrived on that boat early yesterday. The old man, Schwartz, ushered you onto his boat and neither of you left the boat all day and night. No one else was seen near the boat in that time and tonight, boom. And you washed up on shore. What do you expect us to believe?"

"Well," Michael licked his lips, "you don't believe I blew that boat up or I'd be under arrest."

"There's still time for that." Sergeant Fitzgerald opened a bottle of water and took a deep, long swig.

Michael looked up at the ceiling, "Yesterday I was just an IT guy. Can't I go back to that?"

"Where do you work?" Detective Keeling asked.

"In San Francisco."

Fitzgerald put the bottle down. "For *whom* do you work, smart ass."

"The Federal Bureau of Investigations."

"Thank you." Fitzgerald opened another bottle and held it out for Michael to drink. "See how this works?"

Michael nodded his head as he leaned up for the water.

"Just a little." Fitzgerald grabbed the water back from him. "Look, I think I've got out you pretty well sewn up but I need to check for internal injuries."

Michael looked at Detective Keeling.

"If I just got blown up," Keeling nodded at Fitzgerald, "Roberta's who'd I'd want patching me up, pal."

Roberta gave a sheepish grin. "Medic in Iraq."

Michael pulled down his sheet and saw a red spot forming on his right side abdomen.

Roberta pressed her lips together and gave a grunt before groping and pressing around his abdomen. "Hurts to breathe?"

Michael nodded. "Mm hm."

She ran her fingers gently across his rib cage making his nipples harden. His face reddened with embarrassment.

She patted him on the shoulder and lifted the sheet back up. "Broken rib. Probably fractured a couple of them. I should tell you I had to give you some stitches so I shaved a small spot on your head and part of your leg."

"It'll grow back."

"Excuse me." Keeling leaned upright from the dresser and went for the door.

"Where are you going?" Michael asked urgently.

"First I'm going to take a piss, then I'm going to make sure my wife and child are sleeping, then I'm going to circle back and turn the coffee pot back on," Keeling answered as he left the room.

"Thanks Chief." Roberta smiled and looked down at Michael. "You have no idea how lucky you are right now. No idea."

Inexplicably Michael remembered the security signal and said, "You look like a giant Lena Horne in drag."

Roberta reached over and throttled Michael's throat. "Shut the fuck up! I will snap you like a twig Mr. Moto."

"I'm sorry!" Michael's eyes bugged out and he squeaked, "I'm sorry. It's a code. I didn't know."

She released her grip. "What?"

"It's a code we use to identify other agents. The old man taught me. I'm sorry, I just thought...I mean, he knew the code..." Michael indicated Keeling. "I'm sorry, you're very pretty. I didn't mean to insult you. I'm very appreciative. Thank you for patching me up."

"Fuck pretty."

"What are you two doing? What do you want from me? Why didn't you turn me in?"

"How should I know?" Roberta said quietly. "My boss called me and said he needed my help."

"Please believe me, I have no idea what's happening. I really am an IT guy. Yesterday I got roped in or transferred to the FBI fraud division, but apparently it's a *special*," Michael made little air quotes with his fingers, "fraud division. I meet this old guy on a bus and he's all, clandestine, and I go to a boat. There, he tells me this long story about an antique chair and some crazy chick."

Roberta rocked back in her chair and nodded. "Lorna."

"Yeah, and then he tells me what this *division* really does and that he's got all this other information and then the boat blows the shit up. Now he's gone. I mean gone like in little bits gone and I'm in a child's bed. What the hell?"

"Oh boy, you really don't know *anything* do you?"

"No God damn it I don't."

Roberta raised her hand to his mouth. "Hey, watch your mouth."

"I'm sorry but you see my frustration?"

Keeling walked back in with two mugs of coffee and looked at Fitzgerald, "Can he have this?"

Roberta shrugged. "Do you drink coffee?"

Michael nodded.

"Be right back."

Roberta took a sip of the coffee.

"Look," Michael took another gulp of water, "I need to find someone named Elliot. He works in Virginia. That's all I really know. Some guy named Elliot. I don't even know if it's a code name or his actual name."

"Keeling will fill you in on what he knows." She stared at the clowns on the wall and shook her head. "This can't be good."

Keeling walked back in as Michael adjusted himself up on the bed and took the mug of coffee from Keeling. Keeling grabbed a small wooden chair and squatted onto the seat. "Okay, so you're an IT guy."

Roberta put out her hand to stop Keeling. "Chief, I'm gonna stop you right there. He don't know shit. *I* know more than he does."

"God damn it." Keeling spoke louder.

"Hey now." Roberta scolded Keeling.

"I'm sorry Roberta. But we can't catch a break."

"He's knows about the San Jose case," Roberta said.

"But that was like over a year ago. Christ, this is serious."

"I *warned* you once."

"Roberta!"

Keeling looked threateningly at Fitzgerald who didn't flinch. "All I'm saying..."

"Okay!"

"...the Lord's name in vain like that. It ain't my soul I'm worried about..."

"Okay, I'm sorry. Forgive me."

"Don't ask for *my* forgiveness."

Michael pulled back his covers. "I have to get out of here. I have to find Elliot."

Fitzgerald pointed at Michael's nakedness. "Cover that up Fool. You ain't goin' nowhere like that."

They heard a light tap on the door before it opened. Michael yanked the sheet over himself up to his chin.

Detective Keeling's wife, Jennifer, poked her head in, "Getting a little loud gang," she whispered.

Keeling popped up from his seat. "I'm sorry Honey. Go back to bed. We'll be more quiet. I'm sorry."

Keeling sat back down. "Why do you think Schwartz chose you to work with?"

"I don't know. he said he looked at my file, or Elliot did, and my boss just gave me up to them."

"What's in your file? Any special training?" Keeling asked.

"No, I mean, field training - sure. But nothing special - not like ciphers or anything."

"What do you work on in IT?"

"I work on a lot of satellite software and tracking."

Keeling leaned back and looked off into the distance. "Okay. Well, that would make sense."

"Why? Why does that make sense?" Michael wanted to know.

"I knew he was working on something over at Spectorgies. He'd asked me to run the plates on a bunch of cars in the parking lot. I think he had a guy in there. And I also know he didn't know anything about computers. Nothing."

Michael agreed. "He said he didn't even have a computer."

"Which is why he brought you in. But I don't think he worked in fraud." Keeling scratched at his chin stubble.

"No." Michael knew that he could get fired and a lot worse for revealing secrets but made a snap decision to take a chance. "How did you know the signals and counter signals?"

Keeling paused briefly. "Schwartz. I am, was, an informant for them or for him."

Fitzgerald leaned back and started to gather her medical bag. "Mmm hmm. I need to go."

"Roberta sit down. I'm sorry I dragged you into this but," he held out his hands, pleading, "I don't trust anyone else over there anymore." Keeling was talking about the Ohlone Police Department personnel.

"I could have told you that. I never trusted *anyone* over there. Bunch of self serving..."

"Okay, but listen, from what I could gather from Schwartz, what he was asking me to look into and keep an eye out for — a lot of it surrounded the new Spectorgies lab over in the office park and down at their Hayward offices. And the reason he even introduced you to the San Jose case is because someone from that case is now working at Spectorgies."

"Lorna?" Michael asked, still wondering about her significance to all this.

"No, but a good friend of hers named Tim. But also because her sister is Tessa Tollison."

"Oh my God really? She's like — " Michael perked up.

Fitzgerald's hand flew up and waved a long index finger in Michael's face.

"I'm sorry, but did you know she and her father basically invented the vocal recognition, speech control in the micro-technology industries? Well not *invented* but *really* revolutionized them. We use all their stuff — like in everything."

"Okay right, I know who she is."

"And dude, she's *blind*."

"Right, but that's not the point." Keeling rubbed his forehead, what is it with these computer geeks? "Michael, I think there is something that Schwartz needed here. He was very worried about his informant, which had to be Tim. I think maybe if you meet up with him, maybe you can put the rest of it together."

A realization hit Fitzgerald. "Oh, that's why you put up with her. She's connected. 'Cause I would have arrested her ass a long time ago, if you'd let me."

"No, that's not why." Keeling defended himself. "You know that was actually Schwartz's idea. She's kept him in cover operations for the past year. The dentist, the gambling ring, the art theft, all that."

"Cover operations? So all that was just for this guy in the FBI? And they didn't even know about it?" Roberta asked.

Michael explained, "No, just him and Elliot."

"Plus, I kind of like her," Keeling shrugged. "She's useful."

Roberta looked down and begrudgingly added, "Well she's honest, I'll give her that, but *useful*? Those arrests, like the art theft, then they would have just been really small potatoes, right?"

"Nothing to cause heads to turn." Michael admitted. "Schwartz had said his ongoing operation wasn't about making big arrests but to put chalk in the inkwells of the Nazi's."

"What?" Both Roberta and Keeling simultaneously asked.

"His real operation, not anything to do with the cover operations, was to sabotage any elements that were horning in on government territory."

"Stopping them before they actually committed crimes? Like of the treason variety?" Roberta asked.

Michael nodded and put his coffee mug down. "What were you doing at the estuary tonight? How did you know when we got there?"

"Oh, I through in that part about knowing when you got there." Roberta admitted.

Keeling took another sip of coffee. "I keep a sailing boat across the estuary over on the Ohlone side by where you washed up. That's how I met Schwartz, after the San Jose affair, I was having a beer at the Yacht Club and there was something familiar about this guy at the bar. I couldn't put my finger on it though. So we got to talking and he said that *I* looked familiar to *him*.

Anyway, the long and the short of it is, he was talking about getting a new boat and we go out to look at his old boat and he puts on that rug he used to wear when he pretended to be Schwartz." Keeling indicated his head. "For a minute I thought he was a serial killer. I can tell you as a cop, I had never been so scared. But he trusted me. Said he'd had his eye on me for years and we started working together.

"I knew about your meeting with him today. He'd said he was bringing in a specialist for one of his informants. I got off work about 11:00 tonight and swung by to check on my boat. I hadn't been around it for a week and I saw his boat lights on from across the estuary. Which was odd. Even when he was there he didn't leave the lights burning. I could see the lights from his new boat were on too. Which was really weird. So I hung out. Finally, I was getting ready to leave, and boom! That other boat blew up, then his boat. A few minutes later, people start running over and I saw your head bob up in the water and make your way across to where I was. I figured you had to be the specialist or the informant."

Roberta looked at her coffee mug. "I'm gonna need some more coffee. Anyone else?"

"Maybe you should get some sleep Michael," Keeling offered.

The story Keeling told seemed plausible enough and if Keeling meant to do any harm to him, he certainly wouldn't have brought his sergeant in to sew up his leg.

Michael shook his head. "I won't sleep."

"I'll be right back," Fitzgerald left the room quietly.

"I got the feeling that Schwartz had a lot of irons in the pot," Keeling said.

"Me too. But what they all were, I have no idea."

"Well, another thing was this FDMA problem he was working on. But I think he was hoping to train you as his replacement. Grooming you."

"Yeah, maybe. He did talk that way a few times. Kept warning me about pitfalls, stuff like that. Things that he'd learned along the way. What's going on with FDMA?" Michael was still on his guard. He did not want to give away what little he did know, at this point.

"Just that the FDMA has been giving money away to these fly by night emergency services companies who are all vying for a place at the table." Keeling offered.

"And he was gumming up the works for them?"

"I'm not sure. We were going to meet tomorrow and he was going to fill me in. He said he had stuff working tonight. Which I assumed meant you."

"And he was to introduce us tomorrow?" Michael shook his head. "If that's the case then we never got that far. He had said something about giving packets of information to me. Do you know anything about that?"

"Like files? Maybe current operations or cover operations?"

Michael pursed his lips and tried to think back, but all he could picture was the strange outfits Schwartz had worn the day they met. "I keep thinking about that muumuu he was wearing on the boat."

"He definitely liked to dress up as different people," Keeling nodded, thinking back to the various disguises Schwartz wore.

"Yeah. He was a strange guy. I mean, you knew him longer." Michael wanted to know more.

"I don't think he had family. I just got the impression he didn't."

"No."

"Roberta's got three kids."

Roberta walked in with the coffee pot.

"You've got three kids?" Michael asked.

She turned to Keeling. "Why you talkin' about my kids for?"

"Just making conversation." Keeling shrugged.

"Don't be talking about my kids though."

"I'm sorry."

"Just because you want to turn your house into Quantico, ain't got nothin' to do with my kids."

"I'm sorry."

She looked sternly at both of the men and then laughed. "I'm kidding. You should see the looks on your faces. Yeah, I got three, two boys and a girl. The boys are so sweet, but my girl – she'll cut you if you look sideways at her."

A deep thundering rumble began as Roberta finished pouring the coffee into Keeling's mug and Michael had just held up his mug to her. The earthquake hit lurching Roberta forward, spilling the hot coffee all over Michael.

"AAAHHH!"

Roberta lost her balance and landed on top of him.

"AAAAHHH!" Michael was pushing at Roberta, who still held the coffee pot in her hands.

Keeling reached over to grab Roberta off of Michael but couldn't keep his balance and landed across both of them. Trying to regain his footing, Keeling reached over and pulled the curtains off the window and on top of Roberta. Michael squeezed out from under them and scrambled to his feet, standing at the head of the bed.

Jennifer flung the bedroom door to see a naked and beat up Chinese man standing on her daughters bed with Keeling and Roberta tangled in the curtains and bedding. Everything stopped. "What *the fuck* is the matter with you people!"

A head popped up covered in red clown sheeting. "I can explain honey."

But Jennifer pointed at the naked Chinese man. "You. Where are your clothes?"

Michael shook his head.

Jennifer looked at Roberta. "Does he speak English?"

Roberta looked at Michael and back at Jennifer. "No. We were helping him. We found him in the estuary."

"Fine. But that's what the church is for, Roberta – you know that."

"I know, that's what I've been telling him."

Keeling pulled off the sheeting. "Now look—"

"I'm going to go get him some clothes and you're taking him to the church." Jennifer shut the door behind her.

Roberta stood up as Michael crumbled to the bed. "I hurt *so* much."

Roberta's beeper went off and she pulled it out to look at it. "Okay that's it for me. I got to go."

Michael and Detective Keeling watched Roberta stomp out as she mumbled to herself, "...never been so embarrassed –"

The door swung open again and Jennifer plopped a pair of jeans and a sweatshirt on the small dresser, her expressionless eyes never leaving Keeling's gaze.

Keeling turned to Michael and said in a hushed voice, "I don't think that bomb was meant for you. Here." He handed Michael the clothes. "I'll help you get dressed. I think you should go into see someone at the FBI and then go to Virginia or wherever this Elliot is."

"But the old man said the place leaked like a sieve."

"Then go and find Elliot. If you were transferred out of your department then they won't be expecting you back anyway."

Michael thought for a beat. "Right. They won't be."

"And if anyone else thought you were on that boat then they *really* won't be expecting you. I'll help you." Keeling helped Michael put his clothes on. "And don't worry about that FDMA thing. I'll take care of it. We'll get Lorna involved. That way you can have a cover operation when you get back. Here's your wallet."

Detective Keelings beeper went off in his pocket. "Shit," he said looking at it, "I've got to go too. Damn earthquakes. Every 51-50 on the island—"

"What?"

"Crazies."

"No. Where are we going?"

"I'm taking you to the Oakland airport. Hopefully the earthquake didn't damage it. You should fly into New York or, I don't know, North Carolina and drive to Virginia if you can."

Michael looked at him in amazement. "I don't have any shoes!" Michael put his soggy wallet in his front pocket. "Just take me to that hotel on the south end of the island – I'll figure it out from there."

"You sure? I can take you to the airport."

Michael looked in his wallet. "No, I need some cash. Just take me to the hotel. I got it from there."

CHAPTER 3

OLD SINS HAVE LONG SHADOWS

Lorna watched Patience who watched Fortitude who stepped gingerly across Lorna's finished piles of disaster equipment and goods. He sniffed around the pile of cat food bags, picked out a sealed bag of cat treats and pranced off the rug triumphantly. Patience looked up at Lorna.

"You two want an early dinner?" Lorna asked him and made a 'tsk tsk' clicking sound with her tongue. The cats know the 'tsk tsk' sound as a sort of dinner bell. Patience got up from the couch and sauntered into the kitchen, where he sat next to his dinner dish and waited – patiently.

"Fortitude! Tsk tsk!" Lorna went into her office and pulled out her office chair to reveal Fortitude tearing at the plastic cat treat package. "Come here smarty pants." She grabbed the cat by his scruff and slid him over the wood floor. Fortitude held the treat bag defiantly in his mouth as she pulled him up into her arms.

As she placed the bowls of gelatinized chicken mix in front of waiting cats the doorbell rang.

"Hey, I didn't know what to bring but Tim said to just bring a pen." Annie stood on the front porch holding up a ballpoint pen, her hair freshly cut into its usual bob. Even in tattered jeans and a sweatshirt, she looked neat and prim as always.

Lorna squinted at her. "You don't want to do this, do you?"

Annie walked into the foyer. "No. Well, it's not that I don't want the knowledge and to be prepared but I want the knowledge and not to have to go to classes. Y'know?"

Lorna led the way into the living room and plopped down onto the couch. "I'm so tired. I'm sorry – Tim did kind of offer you up, I think. If you don't want to go –"

Annie stopped walking when she got the full scope of the living room. There were piles and piles of bags and packages, backpacks, first aid boxes, clothes, freeze dried food, and tools. "Um," Annie squeaked.

"Here's what happened," Lorna explained throwing her arms up. "I read all the information I could online about disaster preparedness—"

"Oh Lorna," Annie maneuvered around a pyramid of water jugs, "you shouldn't read those things. Sally's going to hit the roof when she sees this mess."

"And I made some lists. Then I crossed referenced them with each other and went over to that dollar store down on Warner and I got half this stuff there, really cheap."

"I don't think that's the point." Annie couldn't take her eyes off the piles. "But it's 5:30 – we should head on over to class."

M. Saylor Billings

Roseanne Featherstone gently placed her hand on her husband's shoulder and gave it a squeeze. "Wake up, Running Bear. Let's have a bite to eat before we go to our meeting."

Running Bear inhaled deeply and rolled over, "Okay Rosie, I'm up." Running Bear got a good look at his wife in the dying sunlight. "Oh you look like a movie star, is that new?"

"No silly, I just rearranged the ribbons." Roseanne patted her thin frame as she flowed out of the bedroom down the creaky wooden stairs. "It's flattering, I think." Roseanne had never been thin and *fit* – she was thin and *malnourished*, and it showed in her graying teeth and thick eyeglasses.

Running Bear picked one of their twelve cats up off the kitchen table as he sat down to eat. "Have you heard from Noah?"

"No. You know, he must have met up with Jimmy. Maybe something happened during the earthquake."

"That wasn't an earthquake – it was a shrug. The earth was just shrugging." He shrugged his shoulders up and down. "I don't know what happened though."

"It was that old bitch Agnes. She had her claws in Jimmy, telling him lies about us," Roseanne said as she waved her fork around. "She's so scared because we represent an alternative for Jimmy and she doesn't like it."

Running Bear nodded.

"What do you think Noah would pay for some dirt on her? Huh? 'Cause I've got the dirt – they never found that first husband of hers. He's probably buried under the porch."

Running Bear locked eyes with his wife and touched her forearm. "Namaste."

"Namaste." Rosie repeated his gesture and closed her eyes letting out a deep breath. "I think it's this meat. It makes me aggressive."

"Then don't eat it. Just have your beans."

"You think he'd pay for that?"

"No. I imagine we'll find out tonight. We'll see Jimmy and ask him what happened."

Sally walked out of her office and stopped by Katie's desk. Of all the people at the HUD offices Katie was *the* person to go to for any San Francisco information. Aside from being the most efficient administrative assistant Sally had ever met, she was also a human yellow pages. Where to go, what to see, what is happening and who was doing what in San Francisco – Katie would know about it. Need to find a Laotian cabbage grater? Katie would know where to get it.

"Done for the day?" Katie looked up from her computer as Sally walked up to her cubilcle.

"I am, a long one too. If I needed to find a radio that had one of those cranks and would charge like cell phone and stuff where would I go?" Sally asked.

Katie threw her head back and stared at the ceiling, her spiky black hair unmoved. "Does it need to be a ham radio or just with NOAA?"

"No, just the NOAA, I guess."

"Big, little, solar, batteries?"

"Uh, I don't know just – little, solar would be cool."

Katie popped her head back down, "You know where the Ferry Building is?"

"Yes. I can take that way home if I take the ferry."

"Okay, as you're walking down Market make a right, um, two blocks past that tourist mall ya' know?"

Sally nodded.

"Go one, no, two blocks and you'll see Ost Marine. They'll have what you're looking for."

"Thanks Katie. There has to be a way for you to get kickbacks from all places you recommend and know about."

"I know. You'd think. See you tomorrow."

Sally turned to leave. She hadn't thought very far ahead on buying a radio. Perhaps she should have looked online for the types of radios that were recommended for emergency responders. It doesn't matter, she thought. Lorna will just be excited that I even thought to pick something out to go into the emergency kit.

The DERT classes were held in the fire department's training facility classroom at the south end of the old military base. The training facility sat next to the Red Cross building and shared a large parking lot. Both single story red brick structures were much newer and a stark contrast to the old dilapidated three story wooden buildings that surrounded them. It would not be hard to imagine the area in its World War II heyday. Even some signage remained on many of the old buildings indicating their purpose.

Wyatt and Charley jumped out of the jeep. Wyatt looked around at the minimally manicured grounds and up to the knocked – out windows of the neighboring buildings. In the setting sun, they seemed more sinister now than it had when he was a kid and rode his bike around the base after school.

Wyatt paused and waited for Charley to catch up. "Look, nothing more. Just say the job didn't work out. If Jimmy asks why, we stick with the truth – Wild Bill was a dickhead. Don't add anything."

"Oh thanks *Daddy*. Actually I was just going to walk in and announce we were collecting intelligence on the DERT operations."

"Fuck you."

"Fuck you, asshole." Charley said as he shoved Wyatt.

Wyatt came back at him and did a stutter step, pumping his fist at Charley.

"Come on Prick." Charley held his arms out to be hit by Wyatt's fist.

Wyatt pointed a thumb at Charley instead. "Hitchhiker."

The private insult between them led Charley to chase Wyatt around the parked cars and up to the classroom door.

Mrs. Pullam pulled her 87 year-old-frame up from the black plush seat and watched her feet as she shuffled to the front of the classroom. "I'm a first responder!"

"Good for you, honey," Roseanne Featherstone called out.

Agnes Strangler rolled her eyes up and looked around the rest of the class. Where the hell is Jimmy? she thought.

Captain Pullam took long strides from the back of the classroom and reached his arms out to his mother, gently taking her by the shoulders. "Not yet Mom. Just a few more minutes."

"Well what the hell are you waiting for?" Mrs. Pullam asked her son.

Captain Pullam mumbled a few words to her as he ushered her back to her seat.

Lorna maneuvered her little red car into the parking lot and looked around at the other cars. "Not many people here," she said as she got out of the car.

"Is that Mrs. Strangler's car?" Annie stared at the faded but pristine yellow Chrysler K Car as Lorna held open the building door for her and shrugged.

They entered through a kitchenette first then through a swinging door that opened to the back of the classroom, where the DERT registration table sat, manned by Ohlone Firemen.

Lorna cast a glance around the room eyeing the other class members as she walked in. People seemed to sit in pairs together at the long tables facing away from the kitchenette. A middle aged Asian man and his son, two old hippies, two college – aged guys, an elderly lady and her middle aged lady, a couple of military rejects, and the impeccably dressed Mrs. Strangler. Mrs. Strangler turned around and waved at Annie. Annie went over to her as Lorna signed herself and Annie to the roster and introduced herself to Captain Pullam.

"Oh. What a nice surprise to see you! My friend Jimmy was supposed to come too but he hasn't shown up. I was afraid they would team me up with that old woman." Mrs. Strangler indicated the Captain's mother, who was struggling to pull on her son's jacket that was four sizes to large. Mrs. Strangler, as always, wore an *haute couture* ensemble.

"Well, I came with Lorna, Mrs. Strangler, but we won't leave you on your own."

Lorna came over and sat down on the other side of Annie. Annie leaned back. "Lorna, this is Mrs. Strangler. This is my friend Lorna whom I don't think you've met."

Lorna reached her hand across Annie. "No we haven't, but I'm pleased to meet you ma'am." Lorna smiled at the neatly dressed elderly woman.

Mrs. Strangler's mouth fell open. "Oh what wonderful manners. I'm pleased to meet you as well."

"I AM A FIRST RESPONDER!"

Lorna's head snapped to the front of the room where she saw Mrs. Pullam plopping back down into her seat.

"Thank you Mother." Captain Pullam combed back long bangs from his forehead as he walked to the front of the room. "House fires, car accidents, tornadoes, hurricanes, earthquakes, floods, tsunamis, choking victims, bike accidents, terrorist attacks – who are the first responders? The fire department? The military? No, it's you. Many of you have already had the Red Cross first aid training and this week we are going to get you prepared – for anything. Now just to be sure, this class is for the section 8 area of the island and, including this class, it will bring Section 8 up to 43 DERT members."

Lorna leaned over to Annie. "I forgot my pen."

"I know some of you had the first aid class together but let's introduce ourselves so we all know each other's names. As you know I'm Captain Pullam. Mom? Will you start us off?"

Mrs. Pullam, who sat at the front in front of her son turned around, "I'm his mother."

Mrs. Strangler leaned over to Annie. "She's a pistol – that one."

Annie nodded her head.

"We're the Featherstones. I'm Rose and this is my husband Running Bear."

Mrs. Strangler leaned over again. "Pfft, his name is *Ronald* and the only tribe they belong to winters in Miami." Mrs. Strangler simultaneously clicked her tongue, winked, and touched her nose.

Annie froze up. She didn't want to respond to Mrs. Strangler's slurs, but didn't know the right words to ask her politely to stop making them.

"I'm Wyatt Murray." Lorna watched the young guy in his late twenties, with hair so thick and black it looked like plush carpeting that had been cut into a military high and tight give a little wave to Mrs. Strangler.

"I'm Charley Ludwig." The young guy next to Wyatt, also in his late twenties, with thinning brown hair, smiled at the group as he looked around.

"I'm Christopher Wu!" The little boy who sat next to his father called out of turn.

Christopher's father smiled at the elderly lady and her daughter who should have been next to go. The elderly lady smiled back at him.

"And I'm Christopher's father, John."

"My name is Carol Suez and this is *my* daughter Judy." Judy's eyes seemed to smile but her chubby cheeks didn't move. Lorna's gaze did not linger on Judy. It was rude to stare at the unfortunate.

The two college aged guys in bad need of haircuts went next. "Craig."

"Ryan."

"I'm Lorna Tollison."

Annie gave a little wave, "Annie."

"Mrs. Strangler."

"Good." Captain Pullam said. "So we're going to be together every night this week and all day on Saturday for the drill. If you can't make it any one of those days you'll have to make it up in the following session before you can be certified and inducted into the DERT program. After that we only ask for two hours a year volunteer time and as you'll see in your three ring binders there are plenty of ways to make those hours."

Lorna looked around and saw that everyone besides she and Annie had a white three ring binder. A dark hand and a long arm covered in the unmistakable police force blue reached from behind Lorna and plopped down a white binder on the desk in front of her. Lorna knew exactly whose hand that arm belonged to but didn't look back. Again the arm reached over and placed a binder in front of Annie. Annie looked back as the Captain continued to speak and said with surprise in her voice, "Oh hi. Thank you."

Lorna had been rendered speechless upon meeting Sergeant Roberta Fitzgerald at the police station well over a year ago now. Roberta struck Lorna as a magnificent creature, a fabled Amazon Woman, with a Foxy Brown afro. But Roberta misunderstood Lorna's stare and speechlessness at that first meeting and treated Lorna coldly. Lorna truly admired Roberta not just for her style, but Lorna thought Roberta had to have stuck through some tough crap to become a sergeant on a predominantly all-male and all-white police force. The heartbreak of Roberta's coldness to her each time they met rendered Lorna unable even to try to put a kind word between them.

Annie leaned over. "There's your hero, Sergeant Fitzgerald."

"Whatever."

"I thought you *wanted her action figure?* Remember?"

Lorna puckered her lips. "Rude people don't get action figures." Lorna ignored the binder and turned her attention back to the Captain who was introducing a man from FDMA.

"Rick Kansas..."

Annie and Lorna quickly leaned in and bumped heads together. Mrs. Strangler leaned around them both and whispered, "Oh, that *is not* his real name."

At the break time, Lorna headed straight for the coffee pot in the kitchenette area. Annie and Mrs. Strangler remained at the table looking through the binders and talking.

"It's good to see you. I'm surprised it took you this long to join DERT. You seem like a proactive kind of person," Sergeant Fitzgerald said smiling.

Lorna looked up at Sergeant Fitzgerald but said nothing. Why was Sergeant Fitzgerald talking sweetly to her all of a sudden?

"Your bud, Keeling, said he might be by too," Fitzgerald continued.

Lorna nodded and took a sip of the steaming coffee. "We're *not* buds."

"Well, he thinks you are."

Lorna shook her head. "Nope. I don't think so. I don't treat my buds like busy bodies or like they're stupid. I don't know of anyone who treats their *buds* that way. So no."

Fitzgerald put a hand on Lorna's arm. "Oh girl, you got it all wrong. Trust me, I'd *know* if someone was being patronizing and that's not it. He just dots all his I's and crosses his T's and he expects that of others. Actually he's said he was really glad you brought all those cases to his attention. We can't be everywhere all the time, y'know. No, he likes you." Fitzgerald leaned her head down to Lorna and said softly, "To be honest, I think he may have been a little embarrassed that it was a regular citizen who got his back on those cases," before lifting her head back up and nodding at Lorna.

"Well that's nice to hear Sergeant Fitzgerald. Thank you."

Fitzgerald rolled her eyes up and laughed. "Please. Call me Roberta. You're all right, you know that?"

"Okay." Lorna smiled back at Roberta, silently accessing her. Too far, Lorna thought. That was a step too far. Call me Roberta? What could she want from me? What is she doing here anyway?

"Sergeant Fitzgerald, it's nice to see you here. Are you part of the DERT?" Annie was craning her neck up in an uncomfortable way. Annie was at least four inches shorter than Lorna, which made her at least six inches shorter than Roberta.

"Hey Annie. No, well, yes the whole department gets trained with the emergency preparedness. But I'm just helping out tonight. We take turns supporting this."

"What's with the cop?" Charley whispered to Wyatt.

Wyatt shrugged and thumbed through the binder.

"The Captain said we'd have to go through the Red Cross first aid class. I said, 'I'm a registered E.R. nurse' and he goes, 'Yeah but it's part of the program.' What a bunch of dumb-asses."

Wyatt looked around. "Keep your voice down Charley. We're supposed to keep an eye on and snuggle up to these people and that FDMA guy Rick. Kansas. That can't be his real name."

"Yeah, you know his real name was like Harry Ball or Dick Wood. So do it, go snuggle up to Rick Kansas," Charley taunted.

"No, he has to come to us. Otherwise it'll look like want something from him. Just be cool. We've got a week."

Charley gulped down the rest of his water and crushed the cup. "Dude, this sucks. I'm going to go talk to Mrs. Strangler, see if she's seen Jimmy around."

Wyatt turned around, catching Mrs. Strangler's eye and waved.

Charley ambled up to Mrs. Strangler's desk. "Hi, Mrs. Strangler, how's your son?"

"As useless as ever Charley. How's your mom?"

Charley was taken aback that she remembered his name. "She's good. She had a knee replacement a while back but now it's as good as new."

"Oh I'm glad. They can replace anything now, can't they."

"Just about. What are you doing in here though? I thought Jimmy said you were hired by those thugs, or whatever he called it, that security outfit."

"Oh, no. They offered but that's not my thing. I'm a nurse. So are we playing poker anytime soon?"

Mrs. Strangler smiled. "Whenever you feel like losing a couple of bucks, come on over."

Annie and Lorna sat back down next to Mrs. Strangler.

"Thanks Mrs. Strangler. Oh, where is Jimmy? I haven't seen him around." Charley asked.

"I don't know. I haven't seen him in a couple of days now."

"Alright then, looks like we're starting back."

"Okay Charley."

Commander Bill White sat at his desk in the grungy trailer and looked about – at the floor, the walls, the desk. He tried mentally retracing his steps. He was not prepared to call his boss at Dragon Logistics and say he had lost his objectives folder. He rubbed his eyes. That morning he had taken his truck and hotel room apart looking for it. He didn't want to think about the other option. The Objectives folder itemized the 'donations' to public officials, the air space feasibility work ups, and the military base renovation plans. Having it stolen was just worst-case scenario. He put his head in his hands. What else had he stashed in that file? And who has it now? Why was this happening to him? Nothing has gone right since he got here. Nothing.

Bill stood up and paced around the small office. He needed to find who had that file. Somebody else had it and I am going to get it back, he growled to himself. He pulled out his cell phone, what was that fat fools name – the one in the brown suit.

When Lorna got home, Sally had already crawled into bed. Lorna put her binder and purse down on the foyer table and latched her keys onto the hook on the wall. On the table sat a wrapped box with a note: *I hope this helps.* Lorna took her shoes off and took the box into the bedroom with her and turned on a reading light. Sally stirred in the bed.

"Hi," Sally said sleepily. "A five and dime store blew up in our living room. Did you see it?"

Lorna laughed. "I'm sorry. I went overboard."

"Did you see my present?"

Lorna held up the wrapped box. "What is it?"

"It's a puppy. Open it before it dies." Sally sat up in the bed as Lorna unwrapped the gift in her usual lightning fashion. Lorna loved presents. And Sally would probably have gotten the same reaction had she wrapped up a box of bandages for Lorna to open.

"It's a box, of something. I can't see it. What is it?" Lorna's voice rose into a high-pitched squeal.

Sally smiled and clicked on her bedside light as well. "Open the box."

Lorna ripped the top off the box and a square black radio fell out. Lorna held it out in front of her. Dials, a crank, an antenna, a lamp, buttons and a solar panel, the casing was softer than metal but it didn't feel like plastic. She held out the box and read off the letters on the side, "LW, SW, SSB, Aircraft, AM/FM, NOAA. What does that mean?" she said excitedly.

"I don't know you'll have to find out," Sally smiled.

Lorna held it up again, "It's a radio. Is it water-proof?"

"Water resistant. Don't get in the tub with it."

"I won't! I love it. Thank you honey." Lorna reached over and kissed Sally. Which was the exact reaction for which Sally had hoped.

"Do you feel better now?" Sally asked.

"I do."

"How was class?"

"Fine. Mrs. Strangler was there."

"Annie's neighbor, that old lady? What was she wearing?"

"I know. She had on a fabulous Jackie O ensemble tonight in green."

"Pearl box hat?"

"No."

"The Fire Chief guy's mom, who's a hundred years old if she's a day, stood up and yelled, 'I'm a first responder!'"

"That's awesome."

"I know. We should all be so lucky."

"Oh and Roberta Fitzgerald was there and she actually made a point to talk to me."

"Sergeant Fitzgerald, the cop?"

"Yeah, came right up and talked to me as if we were old friends like with secrets and shit."

"What'd she say?"

"Oh girl," Lorna impersonated Roberta. "You know Keeling likes you. Thinks the world of you, wishes more citizens were like you. You aw'ight."

"Shut up."

"I'm serious, dude."

"Why?"

"Who knows? Maybe she didn't have anyone else to talk to. Maybe someone made a complaint against her and she's gonna need character witnesses or something."

"How'd she know you were going to be there?"

"She didn't. She was just there to help out." Lorna got off the bed. "Whatever. I love my new radio, honey. Thank you so much."

"You're welcome. I needed to contribute. I can't wait to see what you put in our emergency kits."

"Me too. But it's going to have to wait till tomorrow. I think I'm sleepwalking."

"You are. Come to bed."

"I will. I haven't had anything to eat tonight."

"Oh, I'm sorry. I should have fixed you something."

"No, go to sleep. I'll be there in a minute. Did you lay out your dry cleaning for me?"

"Yes, next to the dresser," Sally mumbled, laying her head back down.

The police cruiser came to a stop next to the White Ford LTD. Roberta rolled down the cruiser window. "Saw your girl tonight."

Keeling leaned his head back. "Aaah, of course! The earthquake this morning! Of course she'd be at the DERT program. What a *very* long day."

"What happened with Michael?"

"Took him to the hotel over on South Shore. He didn't want to go to the airport. I don't know. He did mention something about packets or files that Schwartz was going to give him. Can you imagine? Your first day on a mission and your boss gets blown to bits?"

"Yeah, I can." Roberta said.

Sometimes Keeling forgot that Roberta was in a war before she became a cop.

"Right, sorry. Of course you could, but I don't think Michael is exactly of the warrior class."

Roberta nodded, "Well, no, but we have to give him credit for surviving."

"Oakland and the Coast Guard are handling the boat blasts. So far they're chalking it up to a leaky gas line."

"You're kidding. Mm hmm. Lazy."

Keeling shrugged. "They don't know. It must have looked like it. They've been finding pieces of Schwartz everywhere, asking people at the yacht club to identify the boats."

"They won't be able to. It's just a small boat dock. I think the city owns it."

"I know. I guess his boss or someone might from the FBI come forward. I don't know how the Feds would handle that. So Lorna's joined DERT huh? Finally a break!"

"I don't get it."

"That woman attracts trouble like a kid to candy. If there's some shit going down over there with FDMA like Schwartz thought, she'll fall into it somehow. She's better than an undercover agent because she has absolutely no idea what is going on."

Fitzgerald shook her head and groaned. "I don't know. She seemed pretty lucid to me."

"No, I agree. She's smart. She just doesn't have an agenda and she wants to learn everything," Keeling said as he waved his hands and wriggled his fingers, "especially anything that is *not* her business. You see?"

"Aren't you putting her in harm's way though? I mean some old guy just got blown up."

"Nah, I don't think that had anything to do with the DERT program. No, that's something else. What'd you find out from the FDMA guy, Rick?"

"Nothing, but he and Pullam had words."

"What kind of words? What do you mean?"

"I couldn't hear but Pullam was certainly bent when he left. Stomped all the way to his car. While Rick, the FDMA guy, threw up his hands and shrugged."

"Okay. Thanks for covering for me. I owe you one."

"One?"

"Okay, I get it. Oh yeah, that, uh, security outfit Dragon is going to do a drill over at the base tomorrow."

"Need us?"

"No, I just thought you should know about it. Just in case."

The Disaster Relief Club

CHAPTER 4

DERT BAGS

Battalion Chief Robert Jules heaved out an audible sigh and cleared his throat as he looked through the file Rick Kansas, the FDMA's West Coast Transitioning Manager, had slid across his desk. Chief Jules, or Julie, as everyone called him, was a mountain of a man. Even at his advancing age, the rippling muscles beneath his shirtsleeves pulsed as he read the file. Only recently had Julie shaved off his trademark handlebar mustache. He had learned a long time ago that a handlebar mustache made children giggle instead of scream and run away when they saw him coming.

Rick Kansas tapped his knee nervously as he looked around Julie's office. The walls were decorated with wooden award plaques and commendations. But, Rick noticed, this office was wall to wall littered with children's drawings and handmade macaroni crafts. Several of the pictures were of children crawling all over

Julie and many were with teenagers in football uniforms. Another showed Julie in a tux standing next to a young Down syndrome woman in a prom gown. In one picture, Julie held a teen by the shirt collar against a wall, up off the ground, feet kicking. Rick focused in on the pinched up face of the teen. It was a young Captain Pullam.

"You go to many proms?" Rick asked.

Julie looked up and bristled at Rick who was now standing in front of the prom picture. "I only go to prom with the prettiest girls in town, Mr. Kansas."

Rick sat back down.

Julie closed the file and slammed his hand down on the desk. "So!"

Rick's breathing grew shallow and he began tapping his knee again. This old fart could crush me like a grape, he thought.

"*You* are going to remove the DERT training program out from under the very people who built it up, who deal with this community daily and hand it over to some pseudo, wanna-be-military group. THEN, if I read this correctly, *they* are going to use the trainees as slave labor."

"It's not *slave* labor."

"Unpaid work *is* slave labor."

"It's community outreach."

"Community outreach is getting people their flu shots or cleaning up beaches, Mr. Kansas, not having them construct emergency service *buildings* or restore the naval base."

"But look, Julie, the island's DERT program has great potential and, with the right professionals leading them, the Ohlone DERT program could be a template for cities nationwide."

"You can't ask members of a community to be beholden to a *commercial enterprise*. That's why they pay taxes. This can't be legal."

"The city manager thinks so. So does the civil service board or the city council."

"Civil Service Board?"

"Julie this is good. It's going to free up your men for actual fires should the big one come." Everyone in California has been anticipating *The Big One* ever since the United States Geological Survey predicted that a magnitude 10 earthquake would hit the California fault lines within the next 20 years.

"And what is their plan should *The Big One* come?"

"Evacuation."

"Then why have them restore the buildings on the base? Over forty percent of the people on this island are over sixty years old. That's about twenty thousand *old people*. How would Dragon move them? Where would they take old people?"

"They've got shelters on the mainland. The Dragon triage center would be here on the base. Look Julie, the city council has been looking for ways to make cuts to the budget. The man-hours it takes to run the DERT program puts an already strained budget too far into the red to operate. By hiring Dragon through FDMA, it alleviates the cost of all those man-hours, insurance, and the DERT equipment costs, plus the city will get funding through FDMA as well."

"For what?"

"Security equipment. Homeland Security is handing out funding for most of the local police forces to assist with anti-terrorism. Now the fire departments are starting to get in on the act as well."

Julie shifted the file on his desk. "It always comes down to money, doesn't it? Let the communities fund themselves but the minute you guys start handing out taxpayer dollars. Some *professionals* need to be brought in. Huh?"

The thought of leaving *his* people, in a time of great chaos, at the hands of gun wielding pseudo-military operators made Julie sick to his large stomach. He couldn't walk down the street without some shiny-faced little kid running up to him for a big bear hug and a twirl around. And he'd grown up with most of the older people. They were his teachers and shop owner - but, right now, what choice did he have? He wasn't being given any options – he was being told what was going to happen. The city council didn't have the guts to say it to his face - they sent this pencil necked paper pusher to do their dirty work. Rick Kansas – that probably isn't even his real name, Julie thought.

"So look, Julie," Rick said, breaking the silence, "Dragon Logistics are having a drill tonight around sundown. It's kind of a staging opportunity to show the city council. I'd really like to have you come by, meet their man in charge, and have a look at their operations. What do you think? Can you make it?"

Julie agreed with a nod, but seemed to be far away in his thoughts. Rick took that opportunity to make his escape from within an arm's clutch of Chief Jules.

"It's bad enough you work for them. Must you say their name?" Annie groused.

Tim should have known better, Annie is never in a good mood on Tuesdays. The online marketing company Annie worked for, Creative Strategies or CReST, was having their weekly meeting for the OoOs, the Out of Office Staff, today in Oakland. Annie really liked doing her job, and being able to work from home, but she really hated these meetings. It was like the penance she must pay for enjoying doing her work. Very Old Testament, she always thought.

The meetings, which had been moved from Thursdays to Tuesdays, would always happen in this way: the group would order their lunch, then Jeremy, the owner of Creative Strategies, would make some type of pronouncement or speech. Then they'd go around the table and give their updates for the various clients to which each was assigned. Heather St. James, Jeremy's 'right hand,' would then, invariably, throw a wrench in the works with a change to the client's order, which would have been, up to that moment, unknown to anyone but her. And the client's order would now have to be redone, thereby ruining at least a day's work for someone on the OoOs team. Either that or Heather St. James would supposedly have sent or lost an email with direct orders from the client to the person working on the assignment. Annie never used the word "hate" but she believed Heather St. James to be an evil witch and fantasized about setting fire to Heather St. James.

Tim started again, "Okay, the company that is giving me money in exchange for services rendered, is sending me to Phoenix, again." Tim rubbed his facial stubble and rolled out of bed. He too, liked his work. But because the company he worked for also held defense-contracting subsidiaries, it also meant that he was constantly defending them to his liberal leaning wife.

"You were just there." Annie complained.

"And now I'm going back. Trust me – I don't like living out of a suitcase, sleeping alone, or," Tim paused and lifted up his carry-on luggage from under the bed, "really anyone I work for. Human Resources is a lot about finesse. People don't realize that, but you have to have *some* finesse. These companies they're sending me out to, the people are like bulls in a china shop."

"Oh, I'm sorry Mr. Poopie." Annie sat on the bed and unzipped his suitcase.

Tim smiled at his wife.

"When do you leave?"

"I should leave tonight, but I can take an early morning flight tomorrow and just go straight to the lab."

"You're doing human resources at a *lab*? What kind of lab is it?"

"No, I'm training their human resource department. They've got me doing a lot of training now. Basically training their workers on paperwork protocol, background checks, giving presentations."

"You should just go tonight, I've got the DERT training and I don't get home until around nine o'clock anyway."

"How's that going?"

"It's fine so far. Mrs. Strangler's in it too."

Tim smiled. "That's awesome. Good for her."

"I know. She sits and whispers all the dirt on people to me. She's not politically correct either." Annie smiled and shook her head.

"Mrs. Strangler being naughty? Doesn't surprise me. Oh yeah, I almost forgot – downstairs in the cellar where I've been remodeling—"

"Yeah," Annie laughed and used her fingers to make quote marks, "remodeling. I know that's your man cave. It's okay."

"No, I'm really remodeling it. But don't go down there yet. I've got columns in places, kind of holding up some retaining walls and I don't want there to be an accident. Like the floor falling in."

"Okay."

Tim moved the suitcase off the bed and flopped down next to Annie. "Not in a big hurry this morning, are we?"

"No."

Lorna rolled up a pair of socks and a pair of underwear into the red medical scrub pants and stuffed the roll into a canvas slip-on boat shoe. She did the same for a bra and long sleeve t-shirt in the red scrub shirt and stuffed them into the other shoe. Performing the exact same procedure on the yellow scrubs and placing each pair of shoes into one of the two red backpacks, she pronounced herself finished. She looked at the result of her work: two stuffed backpacks, or "go kits", and two large trash bins on wheels for sheltering in place. Two smaller kits, one for the car and one for Sally to take to work with her, sat on top of the trash bins. Her peace of mind was short-lived. Lorna's stomach turned over, churning for food. She looked at the television clock that read 3:00.

"No wonder I'm hungry."

Lorna got up to go to the kitchen and paused by her office. Was she ready to give it up? All those years building a name for Drugstore Publishing – how much longer before all her contacts in the New York and online publishing dried up? At thirty-three she was no longer a fresh young voice. Trading edgy New York for passive aggressive California had, she would admit, changed her writing voice somewhat. She was less hungry – less aggressive. She could get it back though, if she wanted to get out of her home office more, move in the technology circles, make new contacts. Or should she change what she published? Start writing long-form fiction and turn Drugstore into a blog? Just start syndicating everything?

She shook her head as she folded her sandwich in half and took a bite – so much to think about. The phone rang.

"Hello?"

"What's wrong?" Tessa asked.

"Nothing. I'm eating a sandwich."

"Why are you eating so late?"

"I was busy!" Lorna yelled through a mouthful of bread.

"Did you get your emergency packs finished?"

"That's what I was busy with."

"Are you going to write articles about it?"

"Probably. I don't know."

"C'mon, what's going on?" Tessa could hear the tension in Lorna's voice.

"Tessa, honestly, there is nothing going on. I'm tired a little maybe, but nothing to worry about."

When they were young, before Tessa had been adopted by Lorna's parents and lost her visual abilities – and long before Lorna's mother had died – Tessa had a bad habit of trying to make Lorna's problems disappear. After Tessa became very wealthy this habit got worse. She was not controlling, really, but she just tried to make sure Lorna never wanted for anything. And it was irritating to Lorna. She knew Tessa only meant well but Lyn, Lorna's mom, had taught Lorna to walk her own path and 'carry her own water.'

"Sally got me a present."

"What is it?"

"It's a super radio," Lorna said through a mouthful of food.

"What's a shupiradio?"

Lorna swallowed her food. "No, it's a radio. But it's solar powered with a light. It's got all these settings and you can hear short wave radio on it. It's really cool. I'm going to take it out to the military base before my class tonight."

"What class?"

"My DERT class."

"What."

"DERT. Disaster emergency ready or response, I don't know. It's a class that teaches the community people how to respond to disasters."

"Oh that's a great idea."

"Annie's taking it with me."

"Good for you two. I'm glad you're learning what to do."

"I know. Where's Dad?"

"I have no idea. I think he's absconded with my assistant though. I don't know what they're up to. Last I heard them they were in the back garden arguing about potatoes."

"I thought Perez went home for a few months."

"He's leaving for Christmas and New Year's."

"Oh that's good then. It'll be nice for him. Did you decide when you were coming out?"

"Next month. And I'm coming out for a couple of weeks, I've got some meetings and a conference to go to in Napa Valley."

"Dad coming?"

"I don't know – ask him."

"Is everything alright between you two?

"Sure. Yeah. He's just getting more interested in engineering the garden than in working these days."

"Well, sure. I feel him on that. I'll call him later."

"Okay, enjoy your sandwich."

"Bye."

Tessa pressed the speakerphone button off and faced forward, toward where Quill, Lorna's father, and Perez were sitting and listening to the conversation.

"She absolutely has no idea, does she?" Quill asked.

"Nope." Tessa answered.

Perez shook his head, "I feel wrong. I think this is wrong to do to Meeez. Lorna."

"Just a little longer Perez. When I go out to California, I'll confront Sally. I'll find out if she's still working for the CIA and we'll flush this out in the open."

"Well her parents are certainly still active. And no one knows where they are! What about that Grandmother?"

"Quill, she's 87 years old. I seriously doubt with two wars raging they've got an 87 year old operative in the field."

"You never know." Quill mumbled, rubbing a liver spot on the back of his hand. "Tessa, I don't want my daughters involved with those people, either of you. We sell our technology to them. That's enough. No more!" Quill never raised his voice and it caused Tessa to bristle.

"Well I don't want it either!"

"Quill," Perez said quietly, "sometimes I have to dig way down deep into the root of a plant to take out the rot. Jew see?"

"Yesss." Quill scooted his chair back and lifted it before letting it drop loudly down behind him. "Thank you Perez." He said as he marched out of the room.

Perez watched him leave and waited to hear the door shut, "Theese ees going to geeet messy."

Lorna parked her car in the classroom facility parking lot and got out with her new radio. She pulled on her red backpack and wondered how long the batteries would last on a full charge from the solar power. When she first drove onto the base she could see the military trucks setting up some type of maneuvers near the air hangars on the west side. So she consciously chose to walk closer to the east side hangars. As she wandered around, she began flipping switches and turning dials on the radio looking for a signal.

Jules sat in his truck watching Delores Tam smile and nod approvingly at the black uniform clad Dragon staff, as they set up their gear and temporary tents. A stocky guy was showing her around, pausing and pointing things out to her. Well, thought Jules, at least I knows who's getting paid off on the city council now. After Rick Kansas left his office, Jules vowed to destroy the Dragon Logistics presence on *his* island and began formulating a plan in his head. But to carry out his plan, he was going to have to become that stocky man's best friend. Jules rolled up the window of his SUV and put it in gear. He saw a tall blonde woman with a red backpack wandering around in the road with a black box in front of her. Jules gave a light tap on the horn making her jump to attention. He waved and smiled at her. Her face lit up and scurried out of his path. DERT, he thought. A new class must be starting up.

"But you came back home." Roseanne whipped back a long wayward bang and tucked it under her eyeglass arm.

"Yeah, ya' know, I love Ohlone Island. It'll always be home. But I hope to be able to branch out some, at least. I loved the East Coast and the Carolina's."

"You're a civil engineer?" Running Bear asked switching his weight from foot to foot.

"Yeah." said Wyatt.

"Well, you should be able to go anywhere with that."

"Yeah." Wyatt nodded.

Charley walked up to them carrying his white binder. "Hey. Door not open yet?"

"No." Wyatt responded.

"This is Charley. We graduated the same year from Ohlone High School."

"Hi Charley. I'm Running Bear, my wife Roseanne."

Charley smiled widely at them. "Which tribe?"

Roseanne let out a wild cackle that made Wyatt jump. Captain Pullam's SUV came to a stop behind them in the parking lot.

Both Roseanne and Running Bear spoke at the same time. "The human tribe!" Roseanne threw back her head with another cackle.

"Hey, I think we know another classmate of yours – Jimmy? Uh, Jimmy. What was Jimmy's last name, dear?"

Roseanne slapped his arm. "Marsh. And he's skipping school!"

Charley and Wyatt exchanged glances.

"Sounds like Jimmy." Charley said.

Captain Pullam scooted around the group and unlocked the facility doors. "Early birds, I like that."

"Yeah." Running Bear rubbed his arm where Roseanne slapped it and then playfully tickled at his wife's ribs. Pullam passed around them and unlocked the door. "He was in our Red Cross class and I thought he said he was continuing on with the DERT program." The older woman, Carol, and her dutiful daughter, Judy, made their way past, nodding to everyone. Charley turned and went inside, leaving Wyatt facing Running Bear. "Why don't you two come by after class one night? I've got some great wine I made myself."

"Oh, right." Wyatt was non-committal.

"Jimmy was coming by real regular for a while," Running Bear nodded to the parking lot and said conspiratorially, "probably trying to get away from that old crank."

Wyatt turned and saw Mrs. Strangler wrestling to get her driver's side door open and leapt into action.

Wyatt pulled the K Car's door open with a great creak.

Mrs. Strangler sat in the driver's seat and said, "I'm shrinking or this door is getting bigger." She lifted up her binder from the passenger side and swung her legs out of the car.

"Both," said Wyatt holding out a hand for her to balance herself. "You just need to oil the door.

"It's nice to have such a strapping young man escort me," Mrs. Strangler said, holding onto his elbow.

"It's nice for me too. Girls my age don't want to be escorted."

Mrs. Strangler stopped and looked up at Wyatt. "Sure they do. They just don't want to be called girls. Wyatt."

Wyatt nodded. "Mrs. Strangler, have you seen Jimmy lately?"

"No, I haven't, and I'm mad at him anyway. Just up and left in the middle of the night."

Wyatt stopped walking again, shocked and confused by what she said. "Uh—I—What?"

"He stays with me sometimes. Well, most of the time, since his parents moved to Clear Lake. He stays in my son's old room."

"Oh. Okay. I'm sorry, of course."

"I saw you met Running Mouth," Mrs. Strangler said, changing the subject.

"Yeah."

"Well, stay clear of them. Trust me. No good can come from people like that."

Lorna froze. Was that Santa Claus in a fire department SUV? He looked just like what she imagined Santa would look like: white hair, rosy cheeks and all. She stopped and looked back as the red SUV drove away. A chill ran up her spine as she smiled to herself.

"You never know." She said cheerfully.

The signal she had been following was dying out so she switched the receiver buttons to SW2. Standing in front of another dilapidated hangar, she moved the dial until she heard a faint signal. She walked around the width of the hangar but was losing the signal again.

"Damn it." Lorna looked at her watch, it was going on 5:30 already. She would have to start heading back to the training class soon. She looked down the long side of the hangar and saw a door open. These buildings would obstruct signals, but I'll bet on the inside the signals would be stronger, she thought. These old structures are probably crawling with old signal wires and antennae.

Lorna made her way down the length of the hangar and let herself into the pitch-black hangar, and abruptly turned back outside. She pulled out the headlamp from her backpack, adjusted it on her forehead and went back inside with the radio still garbling.

Glancing around with her headlamp on, she could see that the enormous space was empty except for some turned-over orange pylons. Lorna put her head down toward the radio.

"Oh duh, there's a light here." Lorna switched the radio lamp on but the volume deadened and she switched it off again. Moving forward, she picked up a strong signal.

"Test, test. This is Rover one. Do you read me Rover two?" The radio sputtered to life.

"OO OO yes. Loud and clear." Lorna said to the radio and picked up her step, walking deeper into the cavernous hangar.

"We read Rover Two. Over.

"Rover three, do you copy?"

Lorna's pace quickened as the signal grew. If she found a good signal spot she could check the other –

Lorna bounced off something face first and she landed upright on her knees. It happened so fast that she didn't have time to catch herself. Something had broken her fall into a hole, she thought. How far had she fallen? She couldn't even see the light from the opened door anymore. It took her a brief moment to realize she wasn't actually hurt. The floor must have fallen through. She could see the headlamp shining on the ground. "Shit!" She leaned down and picked it up and placed it back on her head. About six inches away from her eyes, the cold dead face of Jimmy Marsh gapped at her in horror. Lorna gasped and leaned back. She had landed on a dead body. Ice cold terror shot though her veins.

"AAAAAHHHHHHHH!!!!!" Lorna jumped up and out of the hole, stepping on Jimmy Marsh's body on the way out.

"AAAAHHHHHHHHH!" Lorna screamed all the way to the door, into the blinding light, when she ran into someone and bounced off of them onto her butt.

"Hey, hey, hey lady. What are you doing?" The young man had a military look but he wasn't the police.

He wore black cargo pants, a black t-shirt, black cap, and had a pistol strapped to his belt.

"I'm – I was—"

He reached down to help her up but seeing his gun, Lorna scrambled up by herself. "Lady, you're not supposed to go into these buildings. What were you doing?"

"What are *you* doing?" Lorna pointed at his gun and backed away.

"I'm security. Now, come on." The security man moved toward Lorna. She jumped out of his reach, turned on her heel, and gave chase. She felt him grab her backpack but lowered her arms to let it fall off as she ran.

He was on her in a flash and pulled her to the ground. "Stop! Hold it!"

Lorna fought like a rabid animal, not letting him get a grip on her arms as he tried to wrestle on top of her back. She wrapped her long legs around him, pulling him down and off her. She scrambled back to her feet only to have him grab her hand and twist in a botched wristlock attempt.

"My finger!" She yelped and pulled away.

He made another lunge for her and she jutted to the right lifting up her left leg to his gut, making contact. She reached around and unsnapped his gun, pulling it from the holster in one movement. She tossed it as far as she could away from her as she ran full throttle towards the classroom building.

Where the hell was Santa Claus when she needed him?

The Disaster Relief Club

CHAPTER 5

SEARCH AND RESCUE

"Where's your friend?" Mrs. Strangler asked Annie as they sat down together at the table nearest the kitchenette.

"I thought she'd be here already. I saw her car in the parking lot." Annie looked around the room. "I don't know, her partner got her a new radio and she said she was going to try it out, so she's probably just lost track of time." Annie saw Sergeant Fitzgerald walk in and waved. Fitzgerald waved back and began talking with the two firemen standing in the corner.

Captain Pullam walked to the front of the room. "Welcome back. Did everyone sign in?" He paused. "Good. Okay, well we have a lot to cover tonight so let's just get started. Last night we went over the basics ..."

Annie watched Mrs. Strangler, who kept looking back at Sergeant Fitzgerald, tapping her pen, and making groaning sounds. "Is everything okay?" Annie asked.

"Well I'm just not sure." Mrs. Strangler shook her head. "I'm just not sure what the right thing is to do now."

Annie looked behind her when she heard the door opening and saw Detective Keeling walk in and take a seat next to Sergeant Fitzgerald at the sign in desk.

"...hazardous materials. But instead we want to talk to you about possible evacuations and what that would look like for you." Captain Pullam was saying, "So we're going to change the agenda's around from your syllabus."

Lorna jumped into the driver's seat of her car, sweat poured down her face and neck. She inhaled and exhaled deep gushes of air. What the hell just happened? She frantically looked around through the car windows for that man in black. She looked down at her left hand to see her middle finger awkwardly jutting sideways. She gasped for breathe, the pain shot up through her wrist and forearm. She dropped the keys from her left hand into her right. She should get to a hospital. No, she should get home. No, she should stay here – the fire department is here. She reached down in the door pocket and grabbed a bottle of water and drank deep gulps. She leaned her seat all the way back and lay still, staring at the interior roof trying to calm herself. She shouldn't do anything. Just calm down!

Keeling leaned over to Fitzgerald and whispered, "Where's your BFF?"

"Shut it." Fitzgerald hissed back.

Not feeling the least bit calmer, Lorna grabbed a pen and the white DERT binder from the passenger seat, checked her mirrors one last time and made a beeline for the door of the classroom. With focused breathing, she blocked out the blazing pain that pulsed up her left arm.

Calm and casual – keep moving forward, she told herself repeatedly as she opened the door, calm and casual.

She smiled at Roberta Fitzgerald, sitting there all proper in her neatly pressed uniform, and at Keeling, who had dark circles under his buggy eyes. Obviously, Lorna thought, he always acts surprised to see me. Heads turned around and Lorna smiled and mouthed, "Sorry," as she scooted around the kitchenette into the classroom.

Mrs. Strangler and Annie turned to see Lorna enter the room. Lorna had no color in her cheeks or lips. Sweat from her forehead had formed mud thick streaks down her face, ears, and neck. Her haphazard ponytail hung to the side. Her sweater collar had been ripped down off her right shoulder and her left shoulder was cocked up toward her ear. She was covered head to toe in dirt and grass stains. Mrs. Strangler's mouth fell open and Annie's eyes grew larger as Lorna sat down.

"Did you have a hard time getting here? What happened?" Annie said quietly.

"Nothing. I forgot my pen." Lorna gave Annie a pressed on smile.

"Bullshit." Annie said audibly, "You look like you've been playing rugby, without a helmet."

"You don't wear a helmet for rugby." Lorna countered.

Mrs. Strangler craned her head over and gave them a disapproving glance.

Lorna smiled at Mrs. Strangler apologetically and turned her head toward the front of the classroom, opened her binder, and casually placed her cold, throbbing hand on the desk.

Annie didn't take her expectant eyes off Lorna. Something *had* happened. Lorna stubbornly kept her eyes forward as Annie looked down at Lorna's enlarged left hand. "OH! Your hand!"

The rest of the class turned around and looked at them. Lorna stretched the corners of her mouth and gritted her teeth. Captain Pullam stopped talking and looked at Lorna. Her calm and casual plan was falling apart.

Mrs. Strangler stood up and leaned across the table looking at Lorna's hand. "Oh yeah, that's broken. Take a look *at that*." She announced to the rest of the class.

Lorna felt trapped inside herself, unable to move. She shivered as the pain she had suppressed shot up around her neck and ricocheted in her brain.

Christopher jumped up from his seat and ran over for a look at her hand. "Sick!"

Everyone gaped at her expectantly. Keenly aware that Detective Keeling and Roberta were now standing behind her, Lorna sat unmoving, staring ahead with that pained grin on her face.

Annie turned to Mrs. Strangler and said, "Mrs. Strangler, will you take notes for us?" Annie gathered Lorna and her binders and stood up.

"Sure." Mrs. Strangler answered.

Detective Keeling grabbed the back of Lorna's chair and began rolling her backward. Roberta grabbed Lorna's left arm, holding it steady. "Lift your feet up Lorna," Roberta said softly. They rolled Lorna into the kitchenette area, pulled down the metal curtain on the counter and swung the door shut.

Eyes moved to Mrs. Strangler, who pursed her lips and rolled her eyes up.

Captain Pullam cleared his throat. "Okay, well, let's keep moving, as I was saying –"

Lorna's voice reverberated out from the kitchenette. "THERE IS A DEAD BODY IN THE HANGAR! A HOLE IN THE HANGAR! I FELL ON A DEAD BODY IN A HOLE AND HE TRIED TO KILL ME."

Everyone's heads turned back toward the kitchenette. Captain Pullam rubbed his forehead and said, "Okay everyone take five and we'll try back in a few minutes."

"Isn't this the type of emergency we should be responding too?" Christopher asked his father.

"Not this time." His father said aloud.

Mrs. Strangler got up from her seat and followed Pullam through the swinging door into the kitchenette where Detective Keeling was kneeling in front of Lorna.

"Sorry. We'll be out of your way in a minute." Keeling said.

Mrs. Strangler looked to Annie for an explanation. Annie shook her head back.

"Do you want me to call an ambulance over?" Pullam asked.

"No, we've got this, I'll take my squad car." Keeling answered.

"Lorna, can you walk to the squad car?" Roberta asked.

"Yes!" Lorna answered with determination.

"Okay, well get up then." Keeling continued patiently, "You can tell us what happened in the car."

Roberta looked at Annie. "Can you follow us?"

"I don't have a car with me." Annie answered.

Lorna looked at Roberta. "I lost my backpack *and* my new radio."

"We'll get them back, don't worry about that now. Come on." Keeling was leading Lorna out the door by her right elbow as Roberta held Lorna's left arm and wrist steady.

Annie saw Lorna's car sitting in the parking lot. "Lorna, can I drive your car?"

Lorna looked at Annie obstinately. "I don't know, *can* you?"

"Give me your car keys Lorna." Annie said sternly. They stopped for a moment as Annie patted at Lorna's jeans pockets and reached in to grab the car keys out.

Mrs. Strangler marched out of the front door with two small white packets and ripped open the tops of them. "Hold it a minute." She called out.

Mrs. Stangler stood in front of Lorna. "Open your mouth, sweetheart." She said kindly.

Lorna looked down at Mrs. Strangler's withered face.

"Stick your tongue out." Mrs. Strangler said as she reached up and grabbed Lorna by the chin. "Come on now, open up."

Lorna opened her mouth and Mrs. Stangler emptied the packets of the white granules on her tongue. "Now, swallow."

"What was that?" Roberta asked.

"Sugar, it will help with the shock." Mrs. Strangler said.

Roberta and Keeling helped Lorna into the back of the police cruiser.

"Roberta, head on over to —"

"I'm on it." Roberta was half way over to her car as Detective Keeling called back to her.

"Meet us back at Ohlone hospital." He finished as he shut his car door and noticed several of the DERT students standing outside watching.

Annie rolled around on the doctor's stool in the examining room and looked at Lorna's cast. "We're going to need to rent a tow truck and put your cast on it to get home."

"I know. Right? How am I supposed to get this through a sleeve?"

Keeling walked in carrying paper coffee cups and handed one to Lorna. "Here. Light and Sweet."

"Thank you." Lorna took the coffee from Keeling with her right hand, her left sleeve had been cut off and she sat on the examining table with her arm in a sling.

The tall, lanky doctor walked back in with a tiny paper cup and said, "Good you have something to drink, open up."

Lorna opened her mouth and the doctor poured the pills from the cup onto her tongue.

"I've got a couple of pain killers in here for tonight." The doctor continued, "But I wrote you a prescription for tomorrow."

Annie jumped off the stool and took the small envelope and paper from the doctor. "I'll hold them for her. Thank you."

"Okay now then, anything else? That shoulder is going to be sore for a few days, but I think you just wrenched it. If you have anything else just come back, we'll x-ray it. Other than that, as soon as they finish your paperwork you can go."

"Let's go to the waiting area. Is that okay?" Annie asked the doctor.

"Sure."

Annie led Lorna out of the emergency room doors. Keeling stayed back and turned to the doctor. "How long before those pain killers kick in?"

"You've got about 10 minutes or so. Then – " the doctor made a loop around his ear with his index finger and whistled.

Keeling left the emergency room went into the waiting room where Roberta sat with Lorna's red backpack. She stood up when she saw them coming over.

Roberta held the backpack up. "This yours?"

"Yes. Thank you. Where did you find it?" Lorna asked taking a seat.

"Exactly where you said it was." Roberta looked at Keeling and shook her head. "No radio and no dead body."

Lorna looked at Annie for validation. "He had dark hair, stringy."

Annie nodded.

Roberta continued, "We found the hole where you fell. It's an old oil-changing pit. There's a streak of dried blood leading to the drain, so something did happen there, but maybe someone moved the body. It's too earl—"

"*After* I was there." Lorna looked at Keeling, "I'm telling you, there was a body there and I fell on it. So the guy who attacked me must have moved it."

Annie was quick to play through the scenario. "So whoever killed him, saw Lorna go in and then moved the body? Why not just leave it? Why would they reveal themselves to Lorna, y' know?"

"What did the base security company say?"

Roberta answered, "Shift change at six o'clock, we're working on getting the name of the staff that was on the clock during the attack."

"Could you give a description of your attacker?" Keeling asked.

"I think so, but he was really, like non-descript white guy, mid to late twenties, medium build, just under six feet, dark short hair. Wearing all black, military style black cargo pants, t-shirt, hat. He had a gun. I took it from him and threw it as I ran. I was hoping he'd go after the gun and not me."

Keeling rubbed his chin. "Yeah, if he'd known you'd seen the body then he would have gone after you for sure."

Lorna suddenly felt like she was in slow motion. "Did you see my radio?" She asked Roberta.

"No radio." Roberta shook her head patiently watching Lorna's head do a slow circle.

A nurse came over holding a clipboard. "Okay." She handed Lorna's health insurance card back to her and held out the clipboard. "I hope you're not left handed."

"No." Lorna said.

"Just sign at the bottom and initial where I've marked on the pages."

Annie stood up. "Can we finish this tomorrow Detective Keeling, it's nine o'clock and I'm sure Sally's wondering where Lorna is right now."

"Yes, I can stop back by in the morning. Go on."

Roberta stood back up. "Need some help?" She asked Annie.

"No we got it." Annie said and grabbed Lorna's backpack.

Keeling and Roberta watched them leave. "My son can make better arm casts than that. What'd they use, Bisquick?" Roberta said softly.

"Ssh." Keeling admonished her. "They ran out of that fiberglass stuff."

"Here's the thing." Roberta started. "You know that group you told me about that had that disaster drill over on the base tonight? *They all* fit Lorna's description of her attacker. It could have been any of them or anyone who was posing as one of them or someone on the base security team. Plus, we have no missing person's fitting Lorna's description of the body."

Keeling huffed and shook his head eyeing the waiting area. "What'd I tell you? She's like a pig to truffles." Keeling wasn't bragging, he was mad. "And I found something else out. The city council already voted to pull DERT out from under the fire department's control and are *handing* it over to Dragon Logistics. Lock, stock, and barrel."

"Can they do that?"

"Sure. Absolutely. FDMA stuck their hands into DERT a long time ago, when DERT started taking root in a lot of high-risk areas. Now, because of the financial meltdown a lot of towns are looking to make cut backs in the city services. And FDMA and Homeland Security, who are flush with all that war funding, are stepping in, but instead of funding the DERT programs they seem to be farming it out to companies."

"That is so counter-productive."

Keeling rubbed his thumb back and forth across the pads of his fingers.

"So who's getting paid?"

"Good question, but that doesn't concern us right now. Right now we have a possible murder on our hands. Look I'll fill out the paperwork in the morning, I have to get some sleep."

"He didn't say what it was about?" Charley asked Wyatt.

"Nope." Wyatt drove the Jeep into the trailer storage yard and parked behind an Ohlone squad car. "Oh, what the shit is this now?"

"We didn't do anything, right?" Charley looked at the squad car.

"I knew this job was a mistake!" Wyatt slammed his palms on the wheel.

Charley looked up at the dilapidated mobile home that contained Commander Bills' office. "Let's just go in and hear what's going on. It's probably about that drill they ran tonight."

The door opened and a heavyset man in a brown suit stepped out. Charley and Wyatt got out of the Jeep and started walking toward the door. The man looked up at them and nodded. Wyatt nodded back. The man walked behind Wyatt's Jeep and took down the license plate number and walked back to his car. Wyatt clenched his teeth and walk in behind Charley.

"How was the drill Chief?" Charley asked Bill.

"Sit down."

Bill took a deep breath and looked at the water stained roof of the trailer. "You have a problem."

Wyatt could no longer hold back his disgust. He snorted and shook his head.

Charley froze but the Commander ignored it and continued, "One of your DERT bags has something of mine and I want it back."

"Who?" Charley asked.

"Lorna Tollison."

Charley looked at Wyatt. "Is that –?" He began to ask.

Wyatt didn't look at Charley.

"Blonde girl. She broke into a hangar tonight and *attacked* one of the base security guards." Bill answered.

"Why?" Charley asked.

Bill shrugged at Charley's obviously ridiculous question.

"What'd she take?" Wyatt asked.

"She took one of my files. Now, I've filled out a complaint with my buddy at the police department, but it's a company file so it's sensitive and I want to keep it out of the public eye. You understand?"

Charley did not understand. "You want us to ask her for it? Sure."

Wyatt could not believe his friends naivety. "We understand what you're saying Commander." Wyatt stood up.

"Sit down, I didn't excuse you, *Why-IT*."

Wyatt hesitated but sat back down.

"Let me tell you something, this woman is dangerous." Commander Bill was convincingly serious. "I don't know why she'd want to take an Emergency Management file or what she intends to do with it but I do know you need to get it back from her."

Wyatt ignored Bill's finger pointing and watched his neck skin jiggle as he bobbed his head forward, punctuating his words.

Bill continued, "You've got twenty-four hours and after that, if you don't get the file, don't come back here. Now you may leave."

Wyatt stood up and left. Charley blinked at the Commander briefly and followed Wyatt out to the Jeep and got in.

"What the fuck was that?" Charley asked as Wyatt started the Jeep and tore off.

"I don't care anymore, I'm done. He can find his own fucking file."

Annie unlocked the front door of Lorna's house and moved over for Lorna to walk inside.

"Thanks – you." Lorna tripped over the front door jam. The painkillers the doctor had given her were impeding her physical and cognitive abilities.

Sally stuck her head out from the kitchen and grimaced at the sight of Lorna's torn clothes, muddy face, and bandaged hand and sling. "Oh my God, what happened?" Sally met them in the foyer.

Annie looked over at Sally. "Wrong place at the wrong time."

"I lost my radio. I'm so sorry." Lorna slurred.

"She was playing with it in an abandoned hangar and fell into an oil-changing pit. Then a guard or security guy from the base attacked her."

"What? Did they catch him?"

"I fell on top of a dead body. He was dead." Lorna stared blurrily at the fireplace.

Sally held Lorna's arm and looked over to Annie. "What's wrong with her? Is this broken?"

"Very. They gave her painkillers. You should put her to bed, and I'll explain it to you."

"Okay. I was just making some tea, help yourself, I'll be right back." Sally paused. "Actually, will you just bring me the scissors? They're on Lorna's desk. Come on honey. Let's get you set up in here." Sally led Lorna to the bedroom as Annie went into Lorna's office.

"Make sure you tip her." Lorna said in a loud whisper.

"I'm too old to go to jail, Ron." Rose Featherstone poured herself another glass of homemade wine.

86

"No one is going to jail, Roseanne." Ronald "Running Bear" wiped the wine from the corners of his mouth.

"But you know that was Jimmy's body she found. You *know* it was. It's just a matter of time—"

"Damn it Rosie, if you're just going to sit there and fret, do it someplace else. Someone is setting us up. Can't you see that? Go to bed, you're drunk. I have to figure out what to do next."

Annie opened the patio door to let her two Australian sheepdogs into the dining room where they plopped down on their sleeping pads. Ernest, the small one, promptly rolled over and showed her his spotted belly, which she scratched vigorously. Bertram, with one blue eye, waited patiently on his pad for his nightly rubbing. Annie moved over to Bert and rubbed back his ears and face. He bent his head down for her to rub his neck as the doorbell rang. Ernie barked once but bowed his head in regret. Annie looked at the wall clock and wondered who could it be at 10:30 at night. Maybe it was Sally.

Annie opened the door to see Mrs. Strangler standing on her doorstep looking drawn and strained.

"Is your friend alright?"

"Yes, Mrs. Strangler. Come in. What are you doing out this late?"

Mrs. Strangler shook her head. "I'm terribly worried. I don't really know what to do, Annie."

"Come in Mrs. Strangler, have a seat. I'll get us a drink."

"No, I don't want to bother."

But Annie continued moving to her drink cabinet and pulled out a bottle of scotch and a liter of soda and mixed two small glasses for them. She returned quickly and placed the drinks on the coffee table between them. Annie watched as Mrs. Strangler reached over and throw her drink back in one movement and replace the empty glass on the table.

"Aaahh." Mrs. Strangler exhaled loudly. "It's my friend Jimmy. You must have seen him before. He stays with me and does the yard for me."

"Yes, I think so."

"I'm very worried, that body your friend saw —"

Annie stopped Mrs. Strangler by holding up her hand. "How do you know that?"

"Well, the whole place heard her, you couldn't help it. She said, *'there's a dead body in the hangar, he's dead.'* And it had to be the hangar we do our DERT and Red Cross drills in, it's the closest to the classroom."

"But why do you think it's Jimmy's body?"

"The morning we had the earthquake, I checked Jimmy's room and he wasn't there. And he hasn't been back since."

"But Mrs. Strangler—" Annie argued.

"Just listen to me a minute. A while back, Jimmy had applied for a job with Dragon Logistics. Now, I'm not sure about Wyatt but I know his friend Charley applied for it too because they both have their nursing degrees and Jimmy thought he'd be a shoe in."

"Charley? The guy from our class? Why would—" Annie started.

"Now just listen. I guess they didn't get those jobs. Because Jimmy never mentioned it again but I think it gave Jimmy an idea because then next thing I know he's got me enrolled in the DERT program with those horrible Featherstone idiots. And he starts going over to their house and drinking and now he's missing."

Annie didn't move.

Mrs. Strangler was sinking deeper into distress. "I'm so worried they put some ideas into his head and he got into some trouble out there on the base. Maybe with drugs."

"Oh." Annie got up to hand Mrs. Strangler a box of tissues.

"His grandmother, Ruth, was my best friend." Mrs. Strangler broke down.

"Mrs. Strangler, you don't know that was Jimmy. There is nothing to indicate that it was him, nothing at all. I just think you're making your self upset over nothing."

"Here." Mrs. Strangler pulled out a photo. "It's his high school picture, but it still looks like him. Can you show this to Lorna for me? I need to know."

Annie did not have the heart to tell Mrs. Strangler the truth. That the cops went back and there was no body in the pit where Lorna fell. Too many questions and, perhaps, if the body was Jimmy's then it might give her some type of false hope. Annie took the picture and nodded. "I will. I will take it over to her tomorrow."

"Thank you. I don't know if she will still be in our class after what happened. So I just want to make sure it gets to her. I guess I should just go wait by the phone, if it is Jimmy's body then the police will be coming by or Jimmy's parents might call."

Annie stood up holding her glass. "Mrs. Strangler, would you like another? I think I might."

"No, no. I should go. I need to keep my wits about me."

Which was why Annie quickly poured them both double scotch and sodas. "Please, Mrs. Strangler, it's been an awful night. I could use the company." Annie thought, if I liquor up Mrs. Strangler then maybe she will go home and pass out. It was the kindest thing Annie could think to do for her at this point.

Mrs. Strangler threw back her head and gulped down the scotch and soda as Annie sipped hers.

"Okay. Why don't you tell me what happened?" Mrs. Strangler said as she placed her empty glass on the table.

Running Bear got out of his old beat up Volvo station wagon and looked across the estuary. He tried to remember all Noah had said to him. Noah had wanted to find out what Dragon Logistics were up to here on the island. Noah had said that Dragon Logistics were a part of the war machine. Was Noah just winding him up? Did he just use them to get to Jimmy? But if Noah had been just telling them what they wanted to hear, that Dragon Logistics were war profiteers setting up a base here on the island, then Noah's boat would still be here. Running Bear sighed and stared out at the charred remains of the boat slips. Had Jimmy found something and ended up on that boat with Noah? What was that young man's life worth, a piece of real estate?

He got back into his car, turned the engine over and checked the contents of his billfold. He needed some rags, gas, and bottles. It's time to fight the Dragon's fire.

CHAPTER 6

THE WOMEN'S GOLF CLUB

Annie felt a warm tongue licking her face. The last thing she remembered was Mrs. Strangler ranting on about the Featherstones and "their ilk." Bert lifted his paw and nudged her on the chin. An indecent sunbeam crept into her living room and pried open her eyelids, exposing her wretchedness.

"Okay, I'm sorry guys, I'll let you out and feed you." She mumbled at Bert and Ernie who sat eye to eye with her. Slowly, Annie inched her body up, leaning against the back of the couch and let the afghan fall off her shoulder.

A meaty blast of air smacked her as she popped off the canned beef dog food lid and she leaned over the kitchen sink and retched. What had she been thinking? That she could actually *out drink* Mrs. Strangler? Annie put the dishes of dog food on the back patio and backed away quickly. She needed to get over to Lorna's, but first, she needed a shower and a blood transfusion.

Commander Bill slammed on his breaks and skidded to a stop. He looked around the trailer storage yard for signs of life. The abandoned trailers and recreational vehicles stood mute, unable to give him the validation he needed. He got out of his truck and walked around the smoldering remains of his mobile office trailer. The generator he used to run the lights and electronics in the trailer had been taken. He pulled his cell phone from his hip clip and dialed the home office.

"Hi. This is Commander Bill White out in Oakland, is John around?" He paused and looked at his watch.

John, that lazy, waste of space, manager of West Coast Operations came on the line. "Yeah, Bill. How's it going out there in sunny Cali-forn-i-a?"

Bill rolled his eyes. "Foggy. Look, I just rolled up to my office and it's been burnt to a crisp and my generator stolen. You guys didn't get a call from the police or fire department last night did you?"

"No. We didn't. Was it arson?"

Suddenly, it occurred to Bill that this could be a blessing in disguise. "I don't think it was purposeful arson, just vandals. Well, look now we're really close to sealing this thing out here but is there a way I can get some space to work out of?"

"Sure Bill, we'll get you set up. How close are we talking? Would it behoove us to rent out some offices or what?"

"We're about a week out. But I'm thinking just another trailer would be fine, they'll need it further down the line anyway. How soon could we make that happen?"

"I'll get it out to you tomorrow. Do you want the same delivery address?"

"No, I'm thinking closer to the target area this time."

"What all did you lose in the fire?"

"Battle-plans. I thought they'd be safer somewhere in the trailer than with me in a hotel room so—"

"No."

"'fraid so."

"Well at least we know they didn't fall into the wrong hands."

"Yeah." Bill gave a self-conscious laugh.

"We can't send that electronically so I'll over night the file to your hotel."

"I'll call you back with that delivery address for the trailer."

"Let us know when you land that bird, we're itching to get out there."

"Will do." Bill hung up and let out a great sigh. He rubbed the base of his palm over his forehead and farted. "God, I hate this place."

The Ohlone's women's golf club met for their weekly round of golf and teed up at 8 am sharp. The mainly retired group were not competitive per se and their solidarity had recently taken down a land developer. The developer's mistake was underestimating them. He wanted to buy up the small nine-hole area used for teaching the junior kid golf clubs and turn it into condo's. They wanted to continue teaching the junior's. He lost.

Mrs. Jules sat in the golf cart and watched her daughter in law, Glynnis, tee off on the first hole. The shot was low and straight for about 100 yards and rolled to a stop a few yards ahead of Mrs. Jules' own ball. Glynnis climbed back into the cart and continued the conversation. "Oh Julie's very upset about it."

"It'll be over his dead body they set up camp on his island – you know how he is." Mrs. Jules knew her son would not just stand by.

"What can he do if they're working as an extension of the FDMA? There isn't much."

"Well now, *I* don't remember being asked if we wanted them here in the first place." Mrs. Jules said with a gleam in her eyes.

Captain Pullam sat in a state of shock, motionless, in Chief Jules office.

Chief Jules pulled out a brochure. "This is their marketing campaign for the volunteers."

Captain Pullam did not look at the brochure. "Julie, am I being fired?"

"No, absolutely not. Your role as the DERT liaison still stands. But you'll be a liaison between Dragon and the fire department, not with the volunteers. It's merely a supportive role, the hours you spend with them will count toward your community service hours."

Captain Pullam shook his head. "I built the Ohlone DERT program. I trained them. I organized it. I wrote the grants for the money."

Julie nodded. "Yes, you did. It's been your baby from the start, I know that." Julie touched his chest. "But the city council doesn't care."

Captain Pullam stood up. "They'll just leave! The volunteers, they'll walk. What am I supposed to say to them? Thanks for all the training and running the drills and oh by the way, listen to these guys now? Who are these guys anyway? Julie, you've got to do something about this."

"I'm sorry, my hands are really tied this time."

"So where is this Rick Kansas now?" Pullam wanted to know.

"Skipped town. He was just here to insure a smooth transition, make sure the council was on board with this."

"You know that shit face had the balls to try and insult you, *to me*? Yeah. One night after the DERT meeting, tried to drive a wedge between us by telling me I should be in charge – that you were past your expiration date. Mother f—"

"Tommy. Watch your mouth now." Julie stood up and grabbed his car keys. "Let's go for a walk." In Julie's eye's, Pullam was still a wayward youth who needed a firm hand.

"No, damn it. I want answers."

Julie walked around the desk and locked eyes with the Captain and nodded, "Mmm hmmm. I'm glad you feel that way. Come on. I have an errand to run."

Captain Pullam did not fully understand but stood up anyway and followed his mentor out to the Battalion Chief SUV and got in. "Where are we going?"

"Just a little ways, I need to check something over at Memorial Park. I understand they want to put in some new facilities on the west side facing the bay, they want to put in a gazebo on the other side of those tennis courts. Have you heard about that?"

"No." Captain Pullam scowled. What did a gazebo have to do with Dragon Logistics taking over his DERT program?

"Well they are. I'm just wondering if it's going to be feasible and I want your input."

They rode the rest of the way in silence stealing glances at one another. Julie parked the SUV in the Memorial Park parking lot. The fog had burned off and the sun was burning bright in a cloudless sky. A soft sea breeze rustled through the palms and live oak trees that lined the park. They sat across from one another at a picnic table.

"Now listen to me." Julie said. "These Dragon Logistic people are not here to *help* us. They haven't come to this island to lend a *professional* hand in training our citizens. They are here for something bigger. The north end of this island, where the military base sits, is a prime piece of real estate for this area. To say they want to set up a disaster emergency site is insulting to our intelligence. But the problem is someone on the city council, or maybe more than one, is in

Dragon's pocket. That's where this is coming from, not so much from FDMA – that Rick Kansas, he's just a middle man."

"But what do we do about it?"

"Well," Jules cocked his head to the side, "it's no good fighting them. I've been trying to come up with a plan. I put a call into Allen Woods over on the council and I'm waiting to hear back from him. If anyone will play it straight with us it's Allen. I'm a little worried about poaching."

Pullam shook his head. "Poaching?"

"I'm afraid Dragon is going to try and hire some of our guys away because of the cutbacks. I need you to keep an ear out for me at the station. Find out what they're offering, if you hear the guys talking about it try to deter them but don't be obvious about it."

Pullam nodded. "What if they try to poach me? Wouldn't I be the most likely candidate, especially if they don't want the volunteers to leave? It would put me in the perfect position to find out what they're up to."

They both thought for a moment. But Julie shook his head.

"Too risky. These guys are just looking for a toe-hold on the base. No, I'm still thinking on it, for now let's just keep an ear to the ground."

Around noon Annie pulled herself together and jumped in the shower before heading over to Lorna's house. The OoOS meeting yesterday had not been another disaster in a long string of disaster's owing, in part, to Heather St. James being out with the flu or perhaps typhoid. Annie could only hope. She checked her emails and workflow charts and decided she had time to go help Lorna make some lunch. Annie slipped the photo of Jimmy Marsh in her back pocket as she closed the front door behind her. As walked across the street she decided if Lorna was still in pain or seemed very upset she wouldn't bring up the photo. But Lorna is more like a yo-yo, she gets to the end of her string and bounces right back.

"What are you doing still in your robe?" Annie asked, amazed that the usually fastidious Lorna still had some mud streaks around her neck.

"Ever try to put a bra on with one of these?" Lorna held out the ridiculously large cast on her left wrist and hand.

"It's excessive." Annie agreed as she followed Lorna into the house. "So how are you feeling?"

"I'm fine, except the throbbing. But I didn't take anymore of those knock out drops. Whew!"

"I know. That knocked you on your ass."

"Speaking of, you're sportin' a meth-head look yourself. Just sayin'."

"Well, thank you. I guess you don't want that lunch I was going to make you."

"Okay, I take it back you look fresh as a spring daisy. Actually, I'm starving."

"Good. Do you want to eat here or I've got some tuna salad at home."

Lorna walked into the kitchen. "We've got some kind of three bean salad and egg salad and salad-salad."

"Sounds like we're having salad." Annie smiled

As Annie busied herself in the refrigerator, Lorna pulled out some plates and utensils and set them on the table before sitting down.

Annie stopped and looked at the sink. "Are we leaning?"

"Don't ask. So, why do you look so tired today? Was I a nightmare? I mean, I do remember getting home and Sally used *scissors* to cut the rest of my shirt off but –"

"Don't ask. Just be glad you didn't sleep in that bra." Annie sat down. "I explained everything to Sally and then went home but then Mrs. Strangler came over and we had some drinks."

"Oh no."

Annie paused from scooping out the bean salad onto her plate. "Wow. That broad can throw them back!"

"Really?" Lorna was pleasantly surprised.

"And there I was thinking I was doing her a favor."

"Why would you be doing her a favor?"

"She thinks the body you fell on was a friend of hers."

"No this guy was young, like younger than us."

"Yes, her friend was named Jimmy. She and his Grandma were best friends, so he kinda grew up with her. When Jimmy's parents moved to Clear Lake I guess Jimmy pretty much moved in with her."

"Really? I mean that's kinda strange not to strike out on your own."

Annie shrugged. "Do you feel like seeing a picture of him?"

"Do you have one?"

"Mrs. Strangler had his high school picture but I don't want to show it to you, I mean I do, but not if you're not feeling up to it."

"Let me see."

Annie pulled out the picture from her back jeans pocket and handed it to Lorna who studied it and handed it back.

"I don't know. I mean I think it is, but I can't be sure. His face was like this," Lorna opened her mouth and widened her eyes.

"Oh that's horrible."

"Right? It was horrible. Imagine landing on something squishy and then realizing you fell on *that* face."

"Have the police been by today? I mean to ask you any questions?"

"No. They're not going to come by, they think I'm a hysteric." Lorna pulled her arm out of the sling and set her arm on the table.

"You *were* somewhat hysterical but no, I don't think, in general, they think you're a hysteric. And who can blame you? I mean your finger didn't break itself."

"*That* would be hysterical. If all of your fingers had personalities and they all ganged up on like the ring finger because they thought it was lazy."

Annie thought for a beat and joined in, "My fingers would be socialists. All for one and one for all."

"Except your thumbs, they'd be the Ayn Rand's," Lorna held up her right hand thumb and said in a falsetto, "pull your own weight, I had to. You are all weak. Thumbs rule!"

Annie started laughing, "Oh no. I'm so hung over. It hurts to laugh."

"Here, you're probably dehydrated have some more water, want my left over pill?" Lorna took another bite of the egg salad sandwich Annie had made.

"No. I really *won't* be able to function tonight. So do you still want to do this DERT thing? I think it would be okay if you didn't. No one could blame you."

"Oh hell no, I don't scare off that easy."

"What did Sally say?"

"About what?"

"Well when I left she didn't seem to crazy about you going back to the base. I mean, you were *attacked* Lorna."

"Yeah, I was, and I won."

Annie gave Lorna a deadpanned look, then wriggled her fingers at her.

"But you should see the other guy." Lorna said.

Annie continued her finger wiggling.

"Seriously, I scratched the shit out of him *and* I stole his gun."

"I love the fact, I'm sorry but I do, I love the fact that a gun saved your life by you actually throwing it away."

"Hippy."

"Possum eater."

"Not everyone from the south eats possum, ya' know. I did spend most of my adult life in New York City."

"Is possum hard to catch in New York?"

Lorna laughed out as the doorbell rang.

"Who could that be?" Annie asked as Lorna got up to answer the door.

"I'll get it, you enjoy your hippy salad."

Lorna secured her robe and opened the door to see a heavy-set middle-aged man in a brown suit. Standing behind him was the guy who had attacked her last night. She would not have known it was her attacker except the two scratch marks that ran from his forehead to his cheekbone. The two men exchanged glances. The young man nodded and quickly left the front porch.

"Lorna Tollison?" The brown suit asked.

Annie quickly popped her head out from the kitchen but instinctively pulled herself out of sight again.

"Yes."

"I'm Detective Jenkins from the Ohlone Police Department. Could you step outside here for a moment?"

Could he not see she was standing in her robe? "No."

The man stepped onto the door jam grabbing Lorna by the arm cast. Swinging her around, he slammed her against the doorframe in a blink of an eye. He had her wrists strapped together before she could yelp from the pain.

"Don't *fuck* with me missy. I'm arresting you for trespassing, vandalism, and assault and battery charges."

When Annie poked her head back out again he had already ushered Lorna off the front porch and was marching her to the patrol car. Annie scanned the front entry way and saw Lorna's cell phone on the built in cabinets. She grabbed it and hit the number 2, which predictable came up with the name SallyCELL.

Sally answered the call. "Hi Baby, feeling better?"

"Sally, it's Annie. I came over to have lunch with Lorna and the police just arrested her on assault and battery. He already took her away."

"What? Keeling arrested Lorna?"

"No. I don't know who it was."

"Okay, I'm on my way. Do me a favor and find Keeling."

The Trident Diner, est. 1922, sits on the southeast corner of the island off the downtown High Street. At some point or another everyone in Ohlone gathers at the Trident. On Saturday and Sunday mornings it is the place to see and be seen. Politicians and political operatives greet diners while businesspeople wheel and deal over waffles and sausages. Little league photos line the walls along with trophies and ribbons. Charley smiled at his 1990 All Star Little League team photo and took a seat at the counter.

"Aren't you in our DERT class?"

Charley turned around and looked at the older woman who spoke to him, it took him a moment to recognize her.

"Yes. Uh."

"Carol, and my daughter, Judy." Carol moved around to reveal Judy sitting in a booth against the far wall.

Judy squinted a smile at him.

"Won't you join us? We just sat down."

Charley did not want to join them but then he'd have to face them in class for the rest of the week.

"Sure. Thanks." Charley grabbed his menu and followed Carol to their table and sat across the booth from them.

"Hi." He said to Judy.

Judy stared at him dumbly before squinting another smile at him briefly.

"So, are you on your lunch hour?" Carol asked.

"Well, not exactly. I'm not employed right now."

Carol tsked and shook her head. "I know, it's hard all over. What do you do?"

"I'm a registered nurse. I work in ECU's mainly. It's just, well I took one job, it was a private job and that did not turn out to be what I thought it was, so I decided to leave."

"Oh that's too bad. But, we might have a position opening up." Judy could not believe her good fortune. She had prayed to Fatima for this very person - a young man to add to her growing network of Assisted Living Emergency Services, or ALES.

Charley brightened. "Really, where do you work?"

"I run the Portside Assisted Living, over on the edge of downtown."

"Yeah, I know it." The idea of going back to emptying bedpans deflated Charley. "I'll get my resume to you."

"That would be fine. It really helps that you're getting involved with DERT as well. We always look for people who are really involved with the community and have that *extra* training."

"Sure."

The waitress came over to the table. "You guys ready?"

"I'll have the Chef's salad." Carol said. "And she'll have the BLT with a side salad. Two teas."

"Dressing?"

"Ranch for both."

"And for you?" The waitress asked Charley.

"I'll have the Trident omelet and a coffee, please."

"Okay, be right back with your drinks."

Charley changed the subject, "What'd you think of that last night? That chick was kind of crazy, huh?"

"Well, at first I didn't know what to think and then she started yelling about the hangar. See, you shouldn't be in those buildings, it's dangerous." Carol said reproachfully.

"Yeah, but those cops ushered her out quick."

"I've been working on our plans for emergency preparedness at Portside. We're having to revamp a lot of the old ones to meet the new standards the state has passed down."

"That's interesting. I didn't know the state had a hand in that as well, I thought it was just for hospitals and critical care."

"Oh no, no. Every state has their rules and regulations pertaining to nursing homes but the state has really put the screws into us lately. We might as well have our own DERT program, really. I just figured, you know, there is strength in numbers so I want to revamp all the island's nursing facilities emergency standards and head them off before they start with their codes and penalty payments."

"That's a good idea, actually. I could really help you with that. Set up a program for your staff and patients."

The waitress showed up with the coffee and teas. Charley smiled up at her. Today is turning out to be an *excellent* day, he thought.

Lorna rode in silence for the mile and a half car ride to the police station.

Jenkins looked up at her in the rearview mirror. "You're going to have to return that file one way or another."

Lorna leaned forward and bit her lip. She had no idea what he was talking about. She tried to steady her breathing and breath into the throbbing pain in her wrist.

"This is just the beginning of a long and tortured road you're traveling down, missy!"

The pain shooting up from her wrist was excruciating, she leaned forward trying to alleviate the pressure on her left hand. This guy wasn't making any sense and she remembered what Sally once told her. One, never speak to the cops without an attorney present and two, never speak to the cops without an attorney present.

When they arrived at the police station, they entered through the electronic gates and Jenkins pulled Lorna out of the rear seat by her robe revealing part of her chest.

As the cell gate opened, Lorna had breathed into her pain, blocking out the sharp plastic wrist straps cutting into her skin. Another woman, a young, dark Hispanic stood up and eyed Lorna up and down. Lorna cocked her chin up and nodded to her. The young woman came over to Lorna and pulled her robe back around her and knotted the tie. Lorna nodded her head in gratitude to the woman.

Annie paced across the reception area at the Ohlone Police Department. Before she left for the police station, she had called ahead and left a message for Detective Keeling. She sat, glancing down at her watch again. Annie looked though the glass partition behind the reception desk looking for Keeling or Sergeant Fitzgerald.

How bad would it be if she called Sergeant Fitzgerald at home? How many Fitzgerald's could there be in the Ohlone phone book? She knows Keeling's wife, Jennifer, from a book club they had belonged to, and remembered how very seriously Jennifer would not allow

Keeling's work to interfere with their home life. Annie fumbled with Lorna's tennis shoes, he didn't even let her put her shoes on. This is really ridiculous. Where is Sally? Did she take a bus or a cab? Ten more minutes, she'll give Sally, Fitzgerald, or Keeling ten more minutes to get here. If they don't, then she'll reach out to Jennifer.

The cement under Lorna's feet was cold and sticky. She sat down on the cement bed slab, pulled her feet up and crossed her legs. Leaning forward seemed to alleviate some of the pinching from the wrist straps. She put her head down concentrating on the events of last night. She had trespassed, but there was not a "No Trespassing" sign and the door was open. Had she attacked that man? She began to doubt her actions. No, she left and was walking, no, she was running away and they ran into each other then he had grabbed at her. Did he know who she was already? How did the police find her? Why did they not come and get her last night? She knew what was going to happen, she would be finger printed, photographed, and stripped before they would set a – wait a minute, that dumb ass didn't read me my Miranda rights. What the hell was going on? Who was that in that pit? Was she being arrested for murder? No the cop said assault and battery.

Jenkins walked through the outside door that led to the rows of cells and stopped outside Lorna's cell. "Lorna Tollison, you are under arrest for aggravated assault and aggravated battery, trespassing, vandalism and resisting arrest. You have the right to remain silent. Anything you say can and will be used against you in a court of law. You have the right to speak to an attorney, and to have an attorney present during any questioning. If you cannot afford a lawyer, one will be provided for you at the government's expense. Do you understand these rights?"

Lorna looked at the detective. "Yes."

"Do you wish to speak to us now?"

"I want a lawyer."

"I didn't ask if you wanted a lawyer, I asked if you wish to speak to us now."

Lorna looked at the woman standing behind her, before turning back to him, "Quiro un abogado. I want a lawyer."

The detective lifted up his clipboard, wrote something on it, and walked away. Lorna went back and sat on the cement slab pulling her cold feet back up from the floor, and leaned forward. The Hispanic woman's eyes never left Lorna.

Sally leapt out of the cab and took several galloping leaps up the stairs to the Police Department. She eyed the reception area as she walked in but didn't see Annie, who was seated in the alcove behind the front doors. "I'm Sally Thompson, attorney for Lorna Tollison. She was arrested and brought in earlier."

"Okay," the man said. "Have a seat."

Sally looked behind her to see Annie seated by the front window, fretting with a pair of Lorna's tennis shoes.

"Actually this is an emergency. Is Detective Keeling or Sergeant Fitzgerald on duty?"

"No, they aren't. Please have a seat, Ms. Thompson."

Sally took a few steps closer to Annie and began digging in her purse and pulled out a pen and a piece of paper. "Annie, this is Detective Keeling's home address, his wife's name is Jennifer. Tell them there has been a mistake and he needs to get to the precinct immediately before this gets out of hand."

Annie watched the receptionist sneer and shake his head before looking back down at his desk. Sally could see his reaction from the reflection in the window she faced.

"Also call this person." Sally handed the piece of paper to Annie.

Annie looked down at the scrap of paper that read: *Please find Keeling immediately. Then call Lorna's father, his # in L's cell phone.*

"Okay. These are Lorna's shoes." Annie handed over Lorna's tennis shoes to Sally and left.

Keeling hadn't had time for a shower today, he looked and felt disheveled. Jenkins looked up from his desk at Keeling, who was leaning casually against the office door jam.

"What do you care?" Gary Jenkins grunted.

Detective Keeling played it cool and said, "I don't. But I was over at the DERT class last night and I was the one who took her to the hospital. Me and Sergeant Fitzgerald."

"Yeah and?" Jenkins leaned back in his chair. "I've got the complaint here. Read it yourself."

Keeling glanced back over his shoulder as he left the door jam and watched Annie walk into the Police Chiefs office and sit down. He picked up the complaint that said the security guard, Kevin Lawrence, had caught Lorna in the act of trespassing and vandalism. Lawrence attempted to question her when she became violent. The subsequent arrest form read that she also resisted arrest when Jenkins followed up on the complaint.

The resisting arrest part just might be true, Keeling thought. Both files were a strange twist on the story Lorna had told him. And there was no mention of the body Lorna had found in the oil-changing pit. Keeling flipped the pages and saw on the arresting form that the Miranda warning had been issued and the 'accused refused signature'.

Keeling looked up from the paper and at Jenkins who was already filling out another form on his computer. Jenkins must be on the take with someone. He casually plopped the clipboard back down on Jenkins desk and took a step toward the door. "Well, make sure you dot your I's on this one, she's very connected."

"With who?" Jenkins looked up from his desk.

Keeling shrugged. "Who isn't she connected to? Why do you think I personally took her to the hospital?"

"It's a clean arrest, what do I care?"

Keeling looked at his watch. It was a quarter past four. "Have you processed her yet?"

"Pfft," Jenkins gargled. "You got a date with her tonight? I've got twenty four hours, she'll keep." Jenkins chuckled, "She's cuffed in there with Crazy Mona, that'll teach her to fight."

Keeling left Jenkins to his typing and walked out, careful to keep his back turned away from the glass-partitioned wall where Sally stood staring in from the reception area.

"Jenkins." Jenkins phone sprung to life with the Captains voice. "Can you come into my office for a moment? Bring the complaint and arresting documents of a Lorna Tollison with you please."

Jenkins pushed a button on the phone. "Be right there Chief."

"Son of a bitch." Jenkins said standing up and pulling on his "lucky" brown blazer.

CHAPTER 7

CHINESE WALLS

Michael sat on the edge on the pastel green bedspread in the cheaply art deco furnished hotel room trying to sort himself out.

His gaze stopped on silver framed print of a pink and beige conk shell. "This cannot be real." He said aloud.

His leg throbbed, his head hurt, he was exhausted and confused. He longed to be sitting in his office cubicle arguing with his coworkers about who would go on the lunch run. Maybe if he just went into work today like nothing had happened? Why was this happening to him and not Trevor or Sunil? They'd all been working on the same projects. But what if this was happening to them as well? Could someone be killing us off one by one?

Right now, he was physically safe. But in the very near future he would need food, sleep, and money. Keeling had given him a little cash. Michael thought Keeling was probably right – it was possible that for all the FBI knew I could be dead. Michael thought about the other guys in his office, surely he could trust them. He would probably get teased for getting involved in this bullshit. No, probably not. He might trust Trevor, if he was still alive. And he was more than a little wary of calling his boss, or former boss. Schwartz had said his boss had offered him up for this assignment. Michael flopped back onto the bed – he needed a plan. The fact is, he may have bought himself some time coming to this hotel – his thoughts whirled around until the knocking on the hotel door woke him up. Michael stumbled off the bed to the door.

"Housekeeping."

Michael mashed his face to the door. "Come back later please." Michael said watching the maid through the peephole. The maid made a notation on her clipboard and moved the cart forward.

Michael focused his eyes on the digital alarm clock that read, 12:30.

He showered and left the hotel, stopping by the grocery store café for a sandwich before catching a bus into the city. On the bus he thought about what the old man on the boat, Schwartz, had told him about blending in and got off the bus by a hardware store in the city.

Michael outfitted himself with a cheap painters hat and coveralls with the remainder of Keeling's cash. He walked the rest of the way to the street corner outside his apartment in Chinatown and stood watching for most of the afternoon. There was only one way in and one way out of the building and he recognized most of the people who came and went. There didn't seem to be anyone watching the apartment building front doors either. Finally, Michael took a chance, casually walking up to the building and entered. His legs were stiff from standing and the gash that tore up his calf was pounding, but he took the stairs two by two until he reached his second floor apartment.

He stared at the door. No discerning marks, no wires sticking out, no new scratches on the floor. He bent down and looked into the keyhole. Of course he wouldn't see anything – what was he thinking?

"Paranoid much?" He said aloud.

Mrs. Li, his upstairs neighbor, hurried down the stairs carrying bags of trash. "Who are you talking to?" She asked in a high-pitched Chinese.

Michael smiled, watched her go by, and replied in Chinese, "Myself."

"You should have a wife and you wouldn't talk to yourself," she said smiling as she rounded the corner to shuffle down the next flight of stairs.

Michael laughed some more. "You've been talking to my mother."

He jammed his apartment key into the lock and threw the door open, closing it quickly behind him. He leaned against the door. The room was hot and stuffy. Dust particles danced in the setting sunlight around the sparsely furnished room. A drip of sweat ran down Michael's brow and into his eye forcing him to blink away the stinging salt. The room looked just as it did when he left. I can't stay here, he thought.

Michael pulled off his coveralls and saw that his leg had bled through the bandages and onto his sock. There was a ruckus in the hall landing and he froze, listening. Someone was knocking at his door. Michael pulled the coveralls back on and went to the door.

Mrs. Li held out an envelope and said in her high-pitched voice, "Here. This is from the white-devil downstairs."

"Is he still down there?"

"Are you in trouble?"

"No. No trouble."

"He asked if you were home and handed me this. He asked me to give it to you."

"A white-devil who spoke all that?"

"No he spoke in American." Mrs. Li got a good look at Michael. "What happened to your head?"

111

"I had an accident at work. The doctor gave me stitches."

"Maybe that's money then." She handed the envelope to him.

"No, it was my fault. I'm lucky they took me to a doctor."

"You need dinner."

"I ate already. Thank you for this envelope Mrs. Li. I have to go. I'm going to stay with my auntie in Portland for a few days. I have to pack."

"Okay. But you see? You need a wife, Michael."

"Yes Mrs. Li. Maybe I get one in Portland?"

Mrs. Li shrugged and moved on.

Michael shut the door behind her and hustled over to the window and held the envelope up into the sunlight. He pulled out a brochure with 'Virginia is for Lovers' in red across the front. He flipped the envelope around where there was a white travel agent sticker. Michael recognized the travel agent logo from the storefront he passed on the bus, it was about 4 blocks away. It was only going on four o'clock. He had time to shower and pack a bag. His stomach growled.

Michael reached into his closet and grabbed his carry on bag. He threw in a pair of jeans, a shirt, underwear, and socks. He got a butter knife from the kitchen and began unscrewing a wall socket in the bedroom. Reaching his hand into the hole of the wall socket, he grabbed a plastic baggy filled with cash. Cramming the wad of bills in his pocket, he didn't need to count it. It was two thousand dollars, his emergency fund. Slipping into his navy pin striped suit and dress shoes, he looked around the apartment one last time. His gaze stopped on his *Star Wars* DVD collection. It may be the last time he sees this place, he thought morbidly.

Michael casually tossed the grocery bag containing the hat, coveralls, and socks into the street trash bin. He looked at his watch as he approached the travel agents. It was only 4:30 but the agency looked closed. The door was locked so he knocked. A head popped up from the back of the store and came to the front.

"You're late." The dashing and smartly dressed young man said to Michael.

"I'm sorry. My upstairs neighbor, she wants me to marry her daughter."

"Oh tell me about it, honey." The young man flailed an arm up and sashayed behind a desk and opened a drawer.

"Your sugar daddy came by earlier and said you'd be by an hour ago, though."

Michael smiled. "He can wait."

The young man stuffed some papers into an envelope and stuck that envelope into another envelope. "I checked you in, so your boarding pass is inside already. Just show it at security with your I.D."

"He better have booked it through the San Francisco airport, 'cause I am *not* going all the way out to Oakland."

"Mm. Okay?" The young man agreed. "But your flight isn't until 8:30. You got plenty of time."

Michael nodded. "Well, I'm sorry it took me so long to get here. Thanks for waiting."

"Oh girl, your daddy is *generous*. I was ready to wait here till midnight." The young man closed his desk drawer. "Must be niiiiccce," he said coyly.

Michael tried to swish his head to the side and purse his lips together. It was an awkward move and he knew it. He got up and turned around to see an older well-dressed Chinese woman standing at the front door glaring at them.

The young man moved around the desk. "It's just my mom."

The young man opened the door and thanked Michael for the business. Michael nodded and left.

At the airport Michael rummaged through his drugstore purchases and placed the prepaid cell phone, the airline-approved bathroom kit, the paperback novel, and *Connected* magazine in his carry on bag. He lifted his pant leg up and removed the bloodied sock that he had scotch taped to his leg and replaced it with a large wound dressing. He probably should be doing this in the bathroom, he thought while looking around the boarding area. It is kind of gross. He carefully placed the bloody sock and wound care packaging in the drugstore bag and threw it way.

Sitting back down he casually glanced around the waiting area again. A haggard looking couple watched their two small children run around in circles, chasing each other. An elderly woman read her book. Two teenagers stretched out staring at the television. Across the way, people milled about waiting for the boarding call. Taking a deep breath, he opened his fast food bag, he couldn't remember when he was this hungry.

Michael waited until the final call before boarding. He had never flown first class before. He took his seat next to a portly elderly gentleman who rested his hands on his cane in front of him without looking up. Michael pulled out his paperback and slipped his carry on under the seat as he settled in.

The flight attendant came around. "A gin and tonic please." The old man said.

"Orange juice." Michael said.

When she returned she offered the old man reading material but he declined.

Michael pulled out the in flight magazine and opened it up. A slip of thick paper fell out onto the floor but Michael didn't bother with it.

The old man turned to Michael and said in a clear and steady tone, "Pick that up."

Michael did so and looked at the paper. It read: *You are the worst agent I have seen in forty years.* Michael folded the paper down and gaped at the back of the seat in front of him.

"You—" Michael turned to the old man who shook his head and looked out the window.

Michael bit his upper lip.

As they disembarked from the plane five hours later, Michael was still none the wiser as to what was happening. The old man had not spoken to him the entire flight. Reagan National airport was nearly empty at this hour of the morning. He kept a safe distance behind the old man but followed him out of the terminal. Waiting until the old man waved down a black sedan before he approached him again, Michael asked congenially, "Share a taxi?"

The old man sneered at him and opened the back door of the black sedan. "Get in, you fool."

The driver looked in the rear view mirror at Michael. "So this is Crane's protégé?" He asked Elliot.

Elliot nodded slowly. The driver was in his fifties with a bulbous nose and heavy features. "Look Michael, the first thing you should have done was to get out of that area. You should have stolen a car and got the hell out of there."

"I did the best I could." Michael said indignantly.

"It wasn't good enough Michael." The old man said evenly.

"Hey, I'd like to see you two survive being blown up. Why don't you old wise asses tell me what the hell is going on first before you start accusing me of – or better yet, if I'm not good enough then get someone else. How about that?"

The old man continued speaking as if Michael had just pleasantly spoken about the weather, "We'll get you some proper medical care first."

The driver nodded.

Michael shifted his eyes nervously between the two men.

"We have a great deal to go over with you and I would rather you not be in pain in our short time together." He turned his gaze to the driver. "We should bring Christy in."

The driver shook his head. "She's got that baby."

The old man's expression did not change. "How delightful."

Michael walked between the driver and Elliot up a winding path to the front door of an old colonial home. The driver let them into the house and took Michael's bag.

"We've got a room for you." He said as he walked deeper into the house.

Michael followed the old man into the drawing room and sat down on a chair as the old man lowered himself onto the couch. Somewhere a grandfather clock chimed.

"My name," the old man began slowly, closing his eyes, "is Elliot Pickles. I was *killed* in an IRA bomb blast in Ireland in 1982. I am now Elliot McClatchen. I was in charge of the entire fraud division for the FBI for some 30 odd years. A protégé of mine, whom you may have already met, is Wayne Felding. Wayne is in charge of the West Coast fraud division."

Michael felt like a fool for his earlier outburst. "No, I worked in IT."

"It doesn't matter. My East Coast protégé is named Christy Booth. However, you will be working out of the home office here and you will report only to Frank Danvers, whom you met as my driver today. Frank is in charge of any "special" fraud division work. In reporting the cover operations, such as money laundering, illegal gambling, kidnapping and the like you will report those to Mr. Felding. Espionage, anything involving the CIA, NSA, NRO, NGA, etcetera, are reported here to Frank, do you understand?"

Michael nodded.

Frank walked back into the room. "Elliot, Dr. Stritch is on his way and Christy can be here this afternoon."

"Thank you. Have a seat."

"Let me get us something to drink first." Frank walked out again.

Elliot returned to Michael. "Crane explained the fraud cases to you and how they work?"

"Pretty much. I cozy up to the local law enforcement and –"

"No." Elliot cut him off. "You do not *cozy* up to anyone."

"But I'm expected to cold find and run down my own cases, make my own network."

"Yes."

"But the people who found me, a police detective named Keeling—"

"He was an informant of Crane's. I know about him."

"He seemed to know a lot about Crane."

Elliot shook his head. "I didn't even know a lot about Crane. He was a strange man but a very effective agent. The best actually."

"How did you know about the blast? How did you get there so fast?"

"I'll show you after the doctor finishes with your leg."

This caught Michael, how did Elliot know about his leg? But he moved on, "Crane said the cover operations paid for the other ones, these special ones I report to Frank, how does that work?"

"Frank will go over all the paperwork with you. As the head of West Coast fraud, Wayne is going to try to squeeze you for more information about what it is you are working on. Give him false leads, false information, and false ideas. Give him as much deference as you can muster, but you do not report to him. I set up this network with people like Wayne in mind."

"I thought you said he was your protégé."

"He was." Elliot grinned for the first time. "I taught him everything he does not know. And in turn he will teach his protégé everything he does not know."

"May I ask a quick question?"

Elliot nodded.

"Are Trevor and Sunil okay?"

"I don't know who they are. Were they in danger?"

"Well I don't know. I didn't know I was in danger. We'd been working on the same projects, so if someone was coming after us for that — " Michael stopped, watching Elliot nod slowly.

Elliot was two steps ahead of him. "There was no connection to the bomb and your IT projects. Crane had chose you for his own reason's, though God help me I don't —"

There was a knock at the door. Frank stood up to answer it.

"This is Dr. Stritch, we met during the Vietnam War. He is the veterinarian for my sheep." Elliot gave a pleased smile.

A thin and stooped older man walked in to the room carrying an old-fashioned black doctor case and nodded at Elliot. Michael stood up and the doctor walked over to him and looked at the shaved spot with stitches on his head.

"That's not bad Pickles, why the rush?"

Michael lifted up his trouser leg, showing part of the bandage to the doctor.

The doctor nodded. "In the kitchen. Does he speak English?"

"Yes I do." Michael said abruptly.

Whatever it was Dr. Stritch injected Michael with made him feel *great*. Michael no longer felt the constant stinging and throbbing. As a matter of fact, he didn't feel anything below his knee. He knew now that he had been wrong about his initial judgment of Frank and Elliot, they were engaging and interesting men. Michael stared at the upstairs office walls in awe, a multi-colored web of yarn covered two entire walls and half a third in the windowless room. It looked like a psychedelic nest that had been pulled apart one string at a time. Colored pegs pinned color-coated index cards to the ends and at various points along the wall.

Elliot had explained the yarn system and where Crane had worked within the nest. Michael stared at the wall and followed two particular colored strings, the red one and the purple one. "That informer. This one," Michael tapped an index card, "that's a guy named Tim. That's all I know. I found that out through Keeling."

Elliot nodded. "The problem is, someone else got to Tim first, we don't know if it was the NSA or the CIA. But he's reporting to someone. This is a very big problem."

"Why?"

There was a light tap at the door.

"Yes." Elliot said to the door.

Frank held the door open for a small woman with short dark haired woman and big black-framed glasses. She held a baby with a shock of black hair sticking up. "Someone's here to see you."

"Ah Christy, come in. You're just in time." He turned to Michael, "I have babysitting to do Mr. Chan. If you'll excuse me." Elliot pushed himself up from the seat as Christy gave the baby over to Frank.

She addressed Frank, "Everything is in the diaper bag," as Elliot closed the door behind him.

"Michael, I'm Christy. Okay, so where did you guys leave off?"

"I'm Cranes' replacement. I conduct my own fraud cases that I report to Wayne Felding. Wayne is a wanker."

Christy nodded, raising her eyebrows and sat down.

Michael continued, "Frank explained the cover stories and paperwork. I was shown the surveillance system in place for agents under Elliot and the check in procedure. Which explained how Elliot got to me so fast. I have to tell you I find that surveillance to be bulky and outdated. No one uses closed analogue systems anymore. Frank is working on my passports and papers, the histories and cover stories, and paperwork for Wayne. Currently, I am to work on this Spectorgies operation and this one here, the purple one, it has to deal with the Chinese government. And that's all I know about it so far."

She realized immediately, looking into Michael's dilated pupils, he was operating on more than just adrenaline. She looked over at the door and said softly, "You look exhausted."

Michael bucked. "No, I'm good."

It was his truth. I'll bet he feels good, she thought, and cocked a grin at him. "Mm, hmm. Okay well that's good." She opened one of the files on the desk and pulled out a grainy black and white photograph of a balding man of medium build. "Do you know who this is?"

"No."

"That's the man who planted the bomb on Crane's boat and tried to kill you. His name is Pearce, ex-CIA, now employed through a subsidiary of Spectorgies." She pulled out another grainy photo, this man is Tim

Doughall, he is a corporate trainer for Spectorgies, and we believe he also works for the CIA as an informant."

She took the photo's back and closed the file folder. "And here's the deal, we think that this guy Tim, is collecting information from various companies that he does his human resource training in and funneling corporate intelligence back to Spectorgies. Not a big deal, except those companies that Spectorgies send him to just happen to have intelligence contracts within our government — the FBI, the CIA, the NSA – you get the picture. The big problem here is that Spectorgies also has other government contracts, just not *our* government. They have contracts with the Saudi's, China, Russia, and Poland. You see the problem here?"

"Yeah, so everything we know is already known to everyone else basically."

"Exactly."

"But hasn't it always been that way?"

"No. Not like this. Several of the tech companies out west use a lot of cloaking and tracking software that is unavailable to most other countries. And that *Michael* is why we stay analogue. Elliot explained that of course?"

"Yes. Quite detailed and explicit."

"Good. I know you're a techy but it's very important to our operation here nothing digital, nothing online. Why do you think we used colored yarn?"

"I get it."

"Good, because personally, I think that's what got Crane killed. He bought that stupid high tech boat for you and, man, they zeroed in on him like a fly in a spider nest."

"I don't like boats."

"I'll bet you don't." Her eyes grew wide. "I want to veer off this for a moment and talk to you about something else." Christy relaxed back into the chair. "Do you have any questions so far?"

Michael shook his head.

"Okay, look, at this point you should have like 50 questions burning a hole in your seat."

"I don't even know enough, at this point to formulate a question. It's like I've been given a top of the line kitchen with all new appliances but all I know to do is boil water. I don't have any recipes. I don't understand why we aren't going after this Pearce guy?"

Christy rested her elbows on the chairs arms and laced her fingers together. "That is an excellent way to put it. I felt the same way about ten years ago, when I was selected. It's like totally counter-intuitive to FBI training. But for Pearce, he's out of our league, we don't do revenge killing." Christy looked up at the ceiling. "Come to think of it, we don't do physical violence at all."

Michael smiled and nodded.

"Okay, well, see now I know where to start with you. You get we're basically a disinformation source. We make Murphy's Laws true. We find out what the players, people and corporations, are up to. Then access the implications and moving forward from there, we either turn it over to the proper division, let it go, or throw a wrench in their operations." Christy turned conspiratorial again. "Elliot has a wonderful implications chart, it's like a bracket chart following a logic system, very clever. He'll take you through it. My favorite has always been corporate espionage those guys are *ruthless*. Far more than any government I've seen, except maybe the Russians. Everything that the corporations do is always about greed and power. Always, it's a given."

"Well that's what I'm working on now with Spectorgies."

"Oh absolutely, and that's just the tip of the iceberg. Since 9/11 an entire new industry was born. There used to be only maybe eight or nine strings there in Elliot's nest, now look at it, there's got to be at least 50 or 60 there. I don't know how he keeps it straight."

"How do you know where it would all sit on the implication chart?"

Christy shook her head. "That would be a question for Elliot. But I do know that the red index cards are all products of the information industry. Spy ware, if you will, whose satellites track what, where, and who. This one," Christy got up and pointed to a red index card, "is a high-powered microwave device thing that induces an instant blackout in power grids. Imagine the implications if that fell in the wrong hands."

Michael was taken aback. "Or in anyone's hands."

Christy sat back down. "That's for J-39 to figure out. Stay out of J-39's way. They take the lead on most of the cyber wars and if you get even a whiff that they're around then back off."

"Why?"

Christy rubbed her ear in thought. "J-39 doesn't have a specific code of ethics they work from. They get transferred in to a situation whenever some other branch of the services needs special technical advice. It just seems to me – they don't really work with people. It's all in the machines and codes they come up with. So one day they do coding work for the CIA and the next day it's tracking and surveillance for the Secret Service. They probably do more to keep people safe from harm than any other arm in the services but it just seems that without a specific set of human values and with so many masters they could do great harm as well – maybe without even knowing it."

Frank poked his head into the surveillance room. Elliot took off the earphones and turned to him. "Is the baby asleep?" Elliot asked quietly.

"No. She's feeding herself the bottle."

Elliot practically leapt up from his seat. "Good. I want to hold her. Put that headset on, you might learn something."

"And let me just tell you here and now Michael, you are going to mess up. You are going to make the wrong assessments about implications of some corporate intel, actions, or products. It happens, trust me. You learn from it and move on." She pulled out another file indicating an end to their casual tete a tete. "There are a few more players here I want to go though and then give you some objectives. But look, you need to ask questions— what if's, where, who, how—because you won't be seeing us again. This is it. I wouldn't wish this mess on my worst enemy, what you've walked into here. This is as crazy as I've ever seen it."

"Thanks."

"There are only five or six of us working here and usually you have like a year to train with someone, I am sorry for you. I'll give you all the information and Frank will give you all the tips and tricks he's got, but you've got to stay on your toes for the next twelve hours before they fly you back. Then you're on your own."

Michael took a deep breath and closed his eyes. He circled his head from shoulder to shoulder and nodded. "I'm ready."

After Christy finished her briefing with Michael, Frank handed the baby back to Christy. "I changed the diaper myself."

"Thanks. Listen," she looked over her shoulder toward the stairs, "give him a lot of mini-breaks, nothing too long – keep his fight or flight in tact – and he should be good for about 12 or so more hours before he crashes. What'd the doctor say about Elliot?"

Frank shook his head. "Not good and he's refusing treatment."

"But why? It's completely curable. Is that crazy old vet treating him? Where is he getting his information –"

Frank stopped her. "It's his choice Christy."

"Oh sure, he just gets to die and leave the rest of us with our asses flapping in the wind."

Frank opened his mouth but didn't speak.

"Right well I'm off then. Good luck."

Frank followed Christy down the path to her car and opened the car door for her. "Christy, he's making arrangements, no ones ass is going to be flapping anywhere. We'll see you later."

The Disaster Relief Club

CHAPTER 8

CIRCLES DON'T HAVE SIDES

The air in the classroom facility was buzzing. Christopher Wu sat up tall with his knees in the seat of the chair busying himself with his father's cell phone. Judy watched him as she touched her new plush fuchsia sweater. The soft material comforted her as she rubbed her fingertips over the sleeve. Rose and Running Bear came in looking ragged and worn and took their seats.

Rose turned to the rest of the class and asked, "Has anyone heard from our classmate? Is she alright?" She looked pointedly at Mrs. Strangler.

Mrs. Strangler answered. "Last I heard she was fine, they had taken her to the hospital."

Christopher glanced up at the two college students, Craig and Ryan, who were staring down at thick textbooks opened in front of them. Christopher got up from his seat, leaving behind the cell phone, and walked across to the table where the students sat.

"Hi." Said Christopher, giving a little wave with his small hand.

"Hi." They said back.

"Um, last night when that lady started screaming my dad said she was crazy. He told my mom about it and she told me that's why you shouldn't go out by yourself at night."

"I think that lady may have been in pain." The bespectacled Craig said.

"She fell and broke her hand." Ryan explained. "But your mom is right, that's why you shouldn't go out at night by yourself. You should always have an adult with you."

"I know." Christopher said.

Craig pulled his glasses off and crossed his fingers over each other. "Can you do this?"

John Wu kept one eye on his son as he spoke quietly to Carol. Judy watched Christopher cross his fingers. "Then what is the point of carrying on?" John wanted to know.

"I imagine Captain Pullam will make an announcement tonight."

"What a colossal waste of time and resources." John said.

"Not entirely, there's nothing to say we must go along and nothing to say we can't start a new volunteer program."

Annie quietly slipped in the through kitchenette door and slid next to Mrs. Strangler. "I'm sorry I didn't get to you sooner Mrs. Strangler, we had some problems today."

"What did she say?" Mrs. Strangler asked. "Was it Jimmy?"

Annie shook her head. "She said she just couldn't be sure."

Mrs. Strangler touched her string of pearls. "Oh, thank you."

Annie took Mrs. Strangler shriveled hand into her own. "But she didn't say it wasn't. There is still a chance it could be him. Mrs. Strangler, I know this class is important for you but I was wondering, after class tonight, would you come with me? Lorna said she wanted to talk to you and I think it is important that you do."

"Well, what about?"

"I think it's about Jimmy. You don't have to, of course, but it might help."

Mrs. Strangler gathered her notebook up. "Let's go."

"We can do it after class." Annie protested.

"If that girl knows about Jimmy then I want to talk to her."

Charley passed by as Annie helped Mrs. Strangler up and took his usual seat next to Wyatt. "Hey. I tried to call you earlier."

Wyatt looked up from his binder and took his cell phone out. "Oh. Sorry. I had the ringer off."

"I think I got a job." Charley said quietly.

"Where?"

"From that lady, don't look back, okay?"

Wyatt lifted his head. "Okay. Which lady?"

"Carol. The old lady behind us, she runs Portside Nursing Facility. I ran into her at the diner today at lunch."

"That's awesome, dude. Good job. When do you start?"

"I don't know. I'm going to give her my resume tonight."

"You haven't given her your resume yet but she hired you?"

"She all but hired me. She's putting together a kind of DERT program for the nursing facilities on the island and putting in for federal disaster money so I told her I could totally help with that. So it won't be just changing bed pans and wiping asses."

"Charley, tell me you didn't tell her about working for Dragon."

"Why would I do that? Bill hates us. Like he'd give *me* a recommendation."

"That's great man. Look I'm going to go say hi to Mrs. Strangler." Wyatt turned around in his seat and looked for Mrs. Strangler. "Where'd she go?"

"I don't know. She was there when I came in." Charley said looking around the rest of the class.

Sally finished wrapping a towel around Lorna's wet hair and tucked the end of the towel in back tearing out a couple of loose strands.

"Ow." Lorna blinked hard.

"Sorry."

The bath ordeal was finally over. Patience and Fortitude had taken ringside seats on the counter to watch the bath show, and jumped down in unison to lean over the tub to watch the water drain out. It had been an exciting hour for them.

After several failed attempts to wash Lorna's hair in the dirt ringed tub, Sally finally decided it was just easier and more efficient to start the shower and climb in as well – with Lorna's giant arm club.

Sally had seen several large bruises around Lorna's forearms and some forming around her shoulder blades but she said nothing about them. Sally couldn't decide whether she was angry at Lorna for getting arrested, Keeling for not filling out the incident reports in a timely manner, or just tired. After all, it was she who bought Lorna that radio, which led her to using it at the hangar, which apparently led to Lorna's arrest.

As Sally finished drying and dressing herself and began helping Lorna maneuver her cast through her sweatshirt Lorna said, "I'm glad Annie didn't call my Dad."

"Well, after Keeling took over there didn't seem to be any reason. I'm just glad he got there before you got booked, or else there would have been a whole other set of problems to deal with."

"Like what?" Lorna said while combing her hair.

"Well, you'd now have a police record and it practically takes an act of Congress to get that expunged. Even then—" Sally tied Lorna's wet hair back into a bun knot.

"Annie totally gets the award for outstanding performance under duress."

"Come here I need to put some medicine on your wrists." Sally pulled out gauze and antibiotic ointment from a drawer.

Lorna held out both arms, her wrist and forearm were cut up where the plastic straps had bit into her skin leaving bright red streaks of scabs. Sally carefully applied the antibiotic and loosely wrapped gauze around her wrists.

Sally considered while she worked, "You know those release forms are stupid, really. I mean basically it's an admission of guilt for the police department that, in fact, some brutality took place."

"Whatever." Lorna sighed.

"Really, Lorna? Whatever?"

"Yes. Whatever." Lorna gave a waning smile and changed the subject. "Mrs. Strangler is coming over, with Annie. I hope that's okay."

"Sure, but why?"

"Well, because whoever ordered my arrest moved her friend Jimmy's body from the oil-changing pit."

"What? Who?"

"I don't know. That's what I need to find out."

"No, who's Jimmy?"

131

"That's the body I fell on, I'm pretty sure it was that missing friend of Mrs. Strangler's."

Sally's voice rose up, "You could have checked with me on this first, Lorna."

"But I can't. I might need to be bailed out of jail again."

Sally's slammed the drawer shut. "I really, really can't tell you how very, very strongly I am against this."

"I know sweetheart. That's why I didn't check with you first."

"Lorna! No." Sally, who is not at all demonstrative, caught Lorna's full attention. "Now damn it! Last night you break an arm and today you get arrested. You need to step off this, now. You're done."

"It was my finger. This finger." Lorna held up the bulbous cast around her middle finger. She arched an eyebrow at Sally. "I know what I'm doing."

"No. You don't. You don't have any idea." Sally countered.

"What would you have me do? Huh? Sit around and wait to be attacked or arrested again? Fuck that! I will not sit around and play victim!"

Mrs. Strangler and Annie could hear the argument as they climbed the front porch steps and paused.

Annie shrugged at Mrs. Strangler's searching look.

"You are such a child!"

"That happens to be one of my finer qualities!" Lorna screamed back.

"Everything has to be your way." Sally's frustration boiled into contempt.

"No." Lorna said quietly, "It doesn't, or else we'd live on a tropical island and have dolphins as pets. But I am going to find out who did *this*," she held up her broken finger, "what happened to that boy and why." She paused, "With or without *anyone's* help. I won't be a victim Sally. I know you're frustrated with me, I can feel it coming off you like heat. But you have to trust me."

"I'm very frustrated."

"I know, honey." Lorna took sliding steps toward Sally with her sweats stuck up around her knees. "Now help me pull up my pants."

"No." Sally turned and went back into the bathroom.

The doorbell rang. Lorna frantically pulled up her sweatpants and answered the door. "I thought you were coming after class?"

"Mrs. Strangler wanted to come now." Annie said as they made their way into the living room.

Sally walked in. "Hi Mrs. Strangler, I'm Sally, Lorna's partner."

Mrs. Strangler looked up at Sally. "Her partner. What business are you in?"

"No. We're lesbians. Homo's." Sally nodded smiling.

Mrs. Strangler turned to sit down and mumbled to Annie, "I kissed a girl once, 1939."

"In the last two days I've been beaten up and arrested and possibly framed—" Lorna broke off. "I'd like a drink, who else?"

"Just tea." Annie said quickly.

"You sit down and talk to Mrs. Strangler, I'll make a tray." Sally walked past Lorna into the kitchen.

Lorna sat down across from Mrs. Strangler and Annie, who sunk into the couch together. "Mrs. Strangler, I didn't want Annie to give you the news in class, so public like that, but I'm about 99 percent sure that was your friend Jimmy I fell on in the hangar."

Mrs. Strangler gasped.

"I'm so sorry."

"Well, where is he? I should identify the body. I can at least spare his parents that."

Lorna looked at Annie for a moment before continuing, "I don't know. That's the other reason I asked you here. It seems the body was moved after I fell on it."

Mrs. Strangler scowled at Lorna.

Lorna answered the question before it left Mrs. Strangler's mouth. "I don't know. All I know is, the only people who knew about my fall were in that classroom with us."

Annie scooted forward on the couch. "We think someone from the class might have called someone else to have the body moved. Besides the security guard that Lorna ran into no one else could have known about the body. Jimmy, I mean."

Sally kept one ear on the conversation as she put down an ice bucket on the coffee table and hurried back into the kitchen.

"Well then the security guard did it." Mrs. Strangler said. "Why aren't they asking him?"

"It is totally possible, but I'm not real sure about that. I mean he had me arrested today on some bullshit charges. Why would he call attention to what happened like that if he was involved with tampering with a crime scene?"

"Why did you get arrested?"

"He said that I trespassed, committed vandalism, assault and battery and resisting arrest."

"Oh my."

"But I was never booked and they released me."

"But with all that you should be rotting away somewhere."

"But I didn't do any of it. Well, except the trespass but I didn't know it was trespassing, there are no signs and the door was open—"

Something dawned on Lorna, Annie could see the revelation in Lorna's eyes.

"— did Jimmy have any dealings or did he know a guy named Kevin Lawrence or a cop named Jenkins?"

Mrs. Strangler shook her head no.

Sally came in with glasses and cups on a tray and set them down and went back for the bottles of liquor and the tea. On her way back in the doorbell rang and she opened the door.

"Oh hi, come on in." Sally said returning to the living room.

Roberta Fitzgerald stood in the foyer. Patience and Fortitude greeted her at the door so she reached down and gave each a pet on the head. She looked at the women gathered in the living room around the drinks tray quietly assessing them and shut the door behind her.

Annie stood up, but Lorna didn't budge or even acknowledge Sergeant Fitzgerald. Annie watched Lorna throw back her head and gulp her drink. Roberta walked in and addressed Lorna, "Didn't I tell you Keeling liked you?"

"It was a wrongful arrest Sergeant Fitzgerald." Lorna swallowed and put her drink down.

"Girl, he turned on one of *his own* for you today."

Lorna stood up and unwound the gauze from her wrists. "One of *his own*? Look at my wrists. Look at these cuts! That cop frog marched me, practically bare breasted through the police department *and you expect gratitude from me*!"

Sally's mouth fell open. "What?"

"Yeah. Remember I only had my robe on in the morning because I couldn't get a bra on with this thing?" Lorna held up her hand cast. "He yanked me out of the police car by my robe and let it fall open just to make sure my humiliation was complete. So NO!" Lorna was in a full-throated scream, her hands shaking with anger. "I'm a little short on gratitude to the Ohlone cops right now! So if you don't mind I need to solve a murder case for this poor old lady!" Lorna sat back down calmly. "Please leave Sergeant, go sing Keeling's praises somewhere else."

Sergeant Fitzgerald looked around at the other women who gaped accusingly at her. Sergeant Fitzgerald took a step backward and turned to leave.

Sally turned to Lorna. "Why in God's name didn't you say something earlier? I would never have let you sign that release." Sally was beside herself. "Lorna, I—"

"I *said,* whatever. I told you to trust me. It was just a half assed attempt to scare me off. He's a pathetic half human and it didn't work did it?"

Annie shook her head in a silent response.

Roberta stopped at the door and turned back around shaking her head. "No." She said aloud and walked back into the living room. "No, this isn't right. I'm not going to leave. Keeling can't really even touch this case, because it's not a homicide. But I can, I'm not the enemy here. I came by because none of you were in the DERT class tonight. If you plan on pursuing this then you're going to need my help. I know we've got some dirty cops and cops who play dirty, but I'm not one of them." Sergeant Fitzgerald tried to make eye contact with the other women but all eyes were on Lorna.

Lorna shook her head. "I don't know. I have questions I want answered." She looked at Sally who shrugged in deferment. Roberta stood firm.

Lorna continued, "Why were you and Keeling at the DERT meetings? Keeling's a detective, what does he have to do with the DERT program?"

"Nothing. He said if there was something strange going on with the DERT program that you'd find it. He said you're 'attracted to trouble like a kid to candy.' His words exactly."

"He does have a point." Annie agreed.

"Why would he think there was something going on in DERT in the first place?" Lorna asked.

"I don't know exactly, I know it had something to do with Dragon Logistics and the FDMA. He asked me to keep an eye on you."

"But how did he even know I was in the DERT program? That I signed up?"

"He didn't. I saw you there the first night. I'm the one who told him. May I sit down?"

"Yeah, go ahead." Lorna said begrudgingly.

"Hang on," Sally said. "How would he even know there was something going on with Dragon or FDMA? What's *going on* even mean?"

"Look, I don't know. I really don't. I'm just trying to wrap my head around it."

"Have you found Jimmy's body?" Mrs. Strangler asked.

Lorna had almost forgotten she was there.

"Who?"

Annie reached into her back pocket and pulled out the picture of Jimmy.

Lorna said, "That's a picture of the person I fell on in the oil-pit thingy."

Roberta took it and nodded. "We did find dried blood there, but without a body to match it to then there's nothing to compare it with. Plus it takes months and months for that stuff to come back from the lab. It's not like on television."

"I don't understand," Mrs. Strangler said, "if he's already dead why hide his body, why would someone do that?"

"To hide their crime. No body, no crime." Roberta answered.

"Can you check the phone records of the people in the class? Someone had to make a call after I got back." Sally asked.

"Not without a court order. What were you thinking?"

"Well, the only people who knew that I found the body were in the classroom and possibly that guard who attacked me." Lorna said.

"I can check on that guard." Roberta said.

"Hang on, let me make a list of who was in that classroom." Annie got up and walked towards Lorna's office and returned with paper and pen.

"It's those Featherstones. Jimmy had been going over to their house a lot after the Red Cross classes we had together." Mrs. Strangler said.

Sally offered, "It is possible that Lorna interrupted whoever was already there to move the body."

"There was an drill being run by FDMA, they've been helping out security groups who want to horn in on the DERT program. Keeling's been working on that angle."

"You know when Jenkins threw me in that squad car, on the way to the station he said something about a file and that I was going down a wrong road or something."

Roberta remembered Michael and the boat blast and looked concerned. "A file?"

Lorna shook her head. "It was something about a file or that I had taken a file or something."

"What was he talking about?" Annie asked.

"I don't know, I was in a lot of pain and I had my head lowered down so it was hard to hear. All I remember was he said something about I had taken a file and someone wanted it back. When I didn't respond that's when he said something about I was going down a bad road or something like that."

"Okay, well I'll tell that to Keeling when we talk, maybe he'll know something about it or can find out. And if you remember anything else make sure you call one of us. Here." Roberta took out a business card and a pen and wrote something on it. "This is my cell phone. Just call it if you need something or remember something. Keep it with you." Roberta left the card on the coffee table.

Sally leaned back in her chair. "If we can't check the phone records, you're going to have to figure this out the old fashion way."

"What does that mean?" Lorna asked.

"Well, what do we know now?" Sally asked and then answered her own question, "We know that – how many people are in the class Annie?"

Annie looked at her list and counted quickly. "Not counting the three of us there are 10 people."

Sally continued, "So to begin in the first part of the class, in the Red Cross sessions, there were 10 including Jimmy."

"No that's not right there were 12 of us, the Featherstones, the Wu's, Carol and Judy Suez, Craig and Ryan – those college boys, me and Jimmy."

"Well who else joined this second session?"

"That was you two and Wyatt and Charley. They're friends of Jimmy's, but I think they'd had a falling out over those Dragon jobs."

Roberta asked, "Did something happen?"

"All I know is Wyatt and Charley used to come over on poker night a couple of times, we don't play for much ya' know pennies and buttons really. Well, the three of them had a job interview with this Dragon or something like that. Then they stopped coming over for poker and Jimmy never said anything more about it. Now, I thought that Wyatt and Charley got jobs with them but Jimmy didn't so he didn't want to talk about it, so I certainly didn't bring it up. The next thing I know, Charley and Wyatt are in that class with us and Charley says they never took those jobs. So I don't really know what happened there." Mrs. Strangler paused and had a far off look in her eyes.

Annie and Lorna exchanged a subtle glance.

"Jimmy had been going over to those Featherstone's a lot during our Red Cross training. I don't know about that either. He said they made homemade wine. I think they were luring Jimmy over there to get him to do their dirty work."

Roberta did not want to interrupt her flow but asked gently, "What kind of dirty work?"

"Those two are always up to some sort of no damn good. Drugs probably."

Sally spoke up again, "Annie, do you remember if anyone was late to class when Lorna was attacked?"

Annie looked up at the ceiling. "Wyatt and Charley were there, and Wyatt was talking to Christopher. So he and his father were already there. Then Carol and Rose were talking. Those guys, Craig and Ryan. I don't remember."

"What about after we left? Did anyone get on their cell phones?" Annie asked Mrs. Strangler.

Mrs. Strangler shook her head. "I remembered from the Red Cross class about sugar and people in emotional shock, so I grabbed the sugar from the coffee counter and went outside."

"Who could we ask? I mean, who was still in the class?" Annie said.

"I can ask Pullam." Roberta said. "I'm pretty certain the head of the DERT program wouldn't dump a body in a DERT facility, the hangar, and then move it."

"Yeah, but who else would think to do that – in there?" Lorna asked.

"Someone in the DERT class." Sally said nodding.

Roberta stood up. "So, we need to find out who killed Jimmy and who took his body. Doesn't have to be the same parties. Can I use your bathroom?"

"Sure, past the foyer on the right." Sally said.

Lorna was looking at Mrs. Strangler who was still staring at the window with a far of look. "Mrs. Strangler, all this talk must be awful for you. You don't need to be here for this, we can take you home if you want."

Mrs. Strangler shook her head and frowned. "Those God Damned hippies did this! They may not have killed him themselves but they were behind this. You'll see. Jimmy had no reason to be down there at all, he should have been at home playing poker.

Roberta came back out pulling on her heavy police belt. "So I'm going to start with Keeling, find out about this Dragon outfit and the base security then with Pullam about what happened after we left the class."

"I can talk to the Featherstones tomorrow." Lorna offered.

"Are you going to stay in the class?" Annie asked.

"Sure, I don't see why not."

Sally groaned and frowned at Lorna.

"I'll be there with Annie and Mrs. Strangler. Right?" Lorna nodded at them.

Mrs. Strangler and Annie looked at Sally.

"I'm just not comfortable with you going back there, *Lorna*." Sally protested.

"Well then maybe you should come with us." Lorna said.

"You know, I can talk with Carol and maybe Judy tomorrow." Annie changed the subject as Lorna and Sally were staring each other down.

Mrs. Strangler was watching Lorna and Sally with some fascination.

Annie continued, "Mrs. Strangler can you talk to Wyatt or Charley?"

Mrs. Strangler snapped to attention and hissed, "Yes. Of course, I'll squeeze it out of their little asses."

Rose and Running Bear followed the stone path through their back gate and let themselves into the back door.

Rose clicked on the kitchen light and threw off her cape. "They know. I know they know, I can feel it."

"Who knows, Rosie?" Running Bear asked as he heaved off his buffalo hide and put their binders down on the chair.

"Did you notice who wasn't in class tonight?" She asked defiantly.

"Well, yeah, it was those two women. But I think maybe they won't be staying in our class."

"It was Strangler and that woman cop too. I just know that Agnes Strangler is poisoning them against us because we're community activists."

"Why? Why would she do that?"

"Because, we're free and she's jealous of that. She always has been with her Jackie O dresses and her tight ass hair buns. What is she telling them, huh?" Rose flung open the refrigerator door and pulled out a bottle of red wine.

"Rosebud, she doesn't know anything. Jimmy said, remember before he left, he said 'don't worry, Mrs. Strangler doesn't know.'"

"But what about Noah, we haven't heard from *him* either. Don't you think that's odd? He pays us for information about the community service board then Jimmy goes to the base and gets himself killed and Noah is missing? I don't understand it Running Bear."

"Look, I know guys like Noah, he's probably got Jimmy somewhere training him, you know, for missions." Running Bear lowered his voice and glanced around the empty house. He did not want to freak his wife out about Noah's charred boats.

"I don't know Papa Bear. But I don't like how this is turning out, these government contractors, like these Dragon people. They're all ex-military, half of them have the shell shock and the other half are just psychopaths. One of them could have just shot him and left him for dead in that hangar. And who knows what they could have done with Noah."

"Rosebud."

"No, just listen for a minute now we need a story for when the cops come knocking. It was *Noah* that came to us because we were in the DERT program, maybe he was just using us to get to Jimmy? He gets Jimmy to go down there during that secret drill they were having and Jimmy gets bumped off. That woman, the blonde."

"Lorna."

"She goes down there, finds Jimmies body and takes the file we sent Jimmy to get. She gets caught and they try to stop her but she gets away. Now *she's* gone from class. Don't you see the pattern here? Whatever is in that file is dangerous stuff. We need to get it back and destroy it."

Running Bear emptied his glass and poured himself another full glass. "Shit."

"So if anyone asks, we didn't know anything. Jimmy was just some kid from our Red Cross class that seemed to like what we were about y'know, 'cause we're community activists? He came over a couple of times to try our wine and that's it. He seemed like a nice enough kid."

"Look, we don't even know if that was Jimmy she was screaming about."

"Of course it was, Running Bear. She fell in the exact hangar we had sent Jimmy. But we need to make nice with her and let her know what we know too. Let her know we can help her. Get her to trust us."

"What then? How do we get her to trust us without alerting her what we know?"

"We'll have to play it by ear I think. We need to put it out there, let it go into the universe and be open for it come back to us."

"I think you were right the first time Rosie."

"What's that?"

"I'm too old to go to jail. Who would benefit from setting us up for a fall if that was Jimmy's body?"

"Agnes Strangler."

"Oh come on, Rosie. Think. These are higher stakes than a neighborhood vendetta, we're talking about a contract worth million's of dollar maybe. Someone, besides Agnes Strangler, knew we were tight with Jimmy. They must have known about the file too. That girl didn't join the group until the DERT portion, she wasn't even in the class before, someone has to know something. Maybe she knows."

"Running Bear, that's what I'm saying. I think that old cow brought them in and did you notice her two other friends those two boys, What-ever and that Charley?"

Ronald thought for a moment, she did have a point. "What's that saying? Once you have eliminated the impossible, whatever remains, however improbable, must be the truth."

Delores Tam sat behind a large mahogany desk in her home office. Her entire head was purple with rage. Bill sat across from her nodding while he looked over the ransom note and a photocopy of his requisition for Delores' bribery money. The ransom note read: *In exchange for $10,000, I will release this receipt and all evidence of wrongdoing back to you. Friday at the DERT drill. Leave the money in a bag in the place where Dragon Logistics left their last package before the drills begin.*

"So you have no idea. None." She said accusingly.

"I have every idea. I know exactly who is doing this and I'm going to take care of it."

"How? How do you know who sent this? What are you going to do? Pay the ransom?"

"No, we'll catch them. We have plans in place for just these situations."

"What plans?"

"We agree to pay the ransom and then we catch them. I already know who is doing it anyway."

"Who?"

Bill tilted his head and nodded. "No, now Ms. Tam, we'll take care of this, it's not going to find it's way to the press. No one is going to find out about it. I've got men in the police and fire department we're working with already. As a matter of fact she has already been picked up, for something unrelated—"

"She? Who is it?" Delores immediately thought about a recent unfortunate incident involving a now jailed land developer, a *former* city council member, and Ohlone's junior golf club.

Bill shook his head. "I don't want to tell you, you're going to have to trust me on this."

"Trust you? What kind of idiot fills out a requisition form for a bribe?"

"Hey now, hold on. You asked for ten thousand dollars to deliver the council votes, that's fine, but you can't expect a corporation to just hand over that kind of money without some type of record keeping."

Delores did not believe him and made no pretense in her utter disgust, "If this leaks out, Dragon Logistics can forget about this contract, do you understand that? I will have no say in the matter. People find out about this and it's over. I'm out of office and there is no way Dragon Logistics will find its way back onto the island."

"I understand that."

"But if I pull my support now and return your money, I can keep my seat on the council, maybe offer the next security firm a place at the table." Delores leaned back in her chair.

"No. You're not going to do that. We're already in. This is a minor hiccup, someone just trying to make a buck. And you know, who can blame them with this economy."

Bill got up to leave. "I'm glad you came to me with this. The less you're involved the better for you."

Delores Tam watched him leave and picked up her phone.

Driving away in his truck Bill made sure he was out of earshot before releasing a primal scream. He beat the roof of his truck with his fist. "WHYYYYY! WHY IS THIS HAPPENING TO ME! I'm doing Jesus' work aren't I? I make people safer. I make people rich. I help others before myself. COME ON JESUS, WORK WITH ME!!!"

CHAPTER 9

EVERY POT'S LID

The next morning Mrs. Strangler sat at her dressing table, arranging her hair into a bun at the nape of her neck and secured it with bobby pins. She thought about the last time she had seen Jimmy. Did he seem distracted maybe? It took her a moment before she realized she was staring at an old woman in the mirror. When had that happened? The doorbell was ringing. She shuffled out of the bedroom and down the hall to the front door.

"Mrs. Strangler, I'm sorry to bother you so early in the morning." Wyatt was holding a bottle of WD-40. "I was going to fix those squeaky car doors."

"Come in Wyatt. You must have read my mind, I was thinking about you."

"Oh?" Wyatt followed Mrs. Strangler into the kitchen.

"Coffee?" She asked.

"Yes, please. What were you thinking about?"

"I was going to ask about that falling out you had with Jimmy."

"Falling out? We didn't have a falling out. I mean, nothing like that." Wyatt explained, sitting down at the table.

"Oh?" Mrs. Strangler raised an eyebrow at him.

"No. I think his pride was hurt that Charley and I were offered jobs with Dragon Logistics, but there wasn't a falling out."

She finished pouring the coffees and sunk down into a chair at the kitchen table with him. "So how do you like the jobs?"

"Well, those jobs didn't exactly work out. I think Charley is going to be working with Portside Nursing soon."

"Portside Nursing Facility," she paused and looked around. "That's Carol, Carol from our class runs that place."

"Yes, I guess she's putting together a kind of DERT program for the island's nursing facilities."

"Oh she is? Is that why you're here?"

"No. I don't – no – I just came by," Wyatt started but couldn't find the words and simply took a sip of the coffee instead.

Mrs. Strangler lowered her head and looked at Wyatt above her eyeglass frames.

Wyatt shook his head. "I'm worried. I didn't sleep last night."

"What are you worried about?"

"I heard what that woman yelled in class, about a dead body. And you know that I know that Jimmy hasn't been back here since the earthquake. I don't know. It just doesn't seem right. Something's wrong. Was Jimmy working somewhere? Somewhere that maybe I could go look for him?"

Mrs. Strangler held back. There was an odd quality to Wyatt's voice. This young man she'd known since before he could shave wasn't being honest with her. She wanted to blurt out everything she had learned last night, but she shook her head. "All I know is that he had been going over to those Featherstones a lot lately."

"Those people from class?"

"Yes, they were in our Red Cross class and took a shine to Jimmy. I didn't like it much, and I told him that."

"Why would he go over there?"

"Well, I'm sure they charmed him with their stories of sit-ins and all that crap from the sixties," Mrs. Strangler threw up her arms, "free love."

"Oh yeah, you know they asked Charley and I to come over to sample their wine." Wyatt scoffed, "Jimmy is so easily drawn to the most inane shit. Sorry, crap."

"I think he was a little lost actually. I don't know. Why *did* you and Charley join the DERT program?"

Wyatt desperately wanted to tell his old high school teacher everything. About working for Dragon Logistics, that he and Charley *did* have a falling out with Jimmy, that *he* had told Jimmy about the secret files, and that he was afraid his boss had killed Jimmy. This whole thing was like quick sand. Every time he thought he was doing the right thing he just sunk deeper into it. But instead he said, "Well after the job didn't work out Charley and I got to talking and then after the earthquake we decided to join. We thought Jimmy would be there."

"I wish he was." Mrs. Strangler said as she sipped her coffee.

Annie parked her car on the street outside Portside Nursing Facility and sat there thinking of an excuse. She could say she was just in the neighborhood. Or, better yet, she was just in the neighborhood and wanted to ask about the classes she had missed. Oh that's good. She didn't have their phone numbers and maybe they could meet before – Carol and Judy walking out of the facility doors interrupted Annie's thought.

Annie caught up with them as they crossed the street. "Carol!" Annie's melodic soprano voice rang out and Carol turned and waited for Annie on the opposite street corner.

"Oh I'm so glad I caught you. I'm Annie, from DERT?"

Carol looked her up and down. "Yes, I know who you are."

"I'm sorry to bother you in the middle of the street but I was hoping you'd have a minute before class to catch me up on what I've missed. Hello Judy." Annie smiled and nodded at Judy.

Judy's expressionless face did not acknowledge the greeting.

"Well I have time now if you'd like, we were going to lunch at the diner. Judy likes the diner." Carol said without acknowledging Judy's presence next to her.

"Oh sure, that's great, I haven't had lunch either."

The three women walked the half block to the diner, sat in a booth, and ordered their lunches. Annie kept stealing glances at Judy. She's like a caged animal, Annie thought, it can't get to you but it menacingly watches your every move. Maybe she was a mute. Annie had never met a mute before, but wouldn't she know sign language then?

"So how's your friend?" Carol asked as she handed her menu to the waitress.

"She's good, well, better I think she's coming back tonight."

"That's nice, but she'll have a hard time during the final drill, we have to do all stations during the drill. Triage, search and rescue, run the fire hydrants, the whole lot."

"Well, don't count her out, Lorna's got a very strong will."

Judy shifted in her seat.

Carol stopped and turned to Judy. The two had a silent moment together before Carol turned back to Annie. "What was all that about a dead body?"

"Shock." Annie said nodding. "The police went back and they didn't find anything and well, she wasn't exactly coherent at the time."

Annie suddenly realized she was answering more questions then she was asking. And the weirdness of Judy's stare was almost overwhelming for her. "But I was wondering, did you see anyone use their cell phone just after we'd left?"

"No, we had a quick break but went straight back to class. Why?"

Annie's brain scrambled. "It's not really related, but you know Jimmy? He's friends with Mrs. Strangler?"

"Yes, he was in the Red Cross sessions."

"Well, he's missing. We think. And someone tried to call him just after we left."

"How do you know?"

"Phone records."

"Well then they'd be able to trace who called." Carol countered.

"No, it was a pre-paid number."

"Why do they think it was someone from our class?"

This is turning into a disaster, Annie thought. "We don't. We're just trying to get a bead on who all knew Jimmy. I mean know him, acquaintances, work friends."

Carol nodded. "Uh huh. Well I'm afraid I don't know anything about that."

Annie wanted to leave. But she stood up and said, "I need to go wash my hands before I eat, I'll be right back."

She went into the bathroom, took deep breaths, and washed her hands. She closed her eyes and let the water run over her hands for a moment before looking back up into the mirror. Judy's dead gaze from behind her sent her bolting head first into the mirror. Judy reached around her and turned the faucet back on without acknowledging Annie. Annie dried her hands and left the bathroom. On her way back to the booth, it dawned on her that Judy was heavily medicated. It was like Judy's emotions, facial expressions, and reactions were simply flat-lined.

"I've been trying to get her to wash her hands before meals for years and you mention it once and she immediately washes her hands." Carol smiled and shrugged. "Kids."

Except your "kid" is pushing forty, and you've medicated her into submission. Annie thought.

"So." Carol waited while the waitress placed their food on the table, "You know about this Dragon Logistics fiasco?"

"No, Dragon what?" Annie lied.

"Dragon Logistics, they're an emergency services contractor for FDMA."

"Oh, no. What about them?" Now I'm getting somewhere Annie thought.

"They're trying to horn in on the DERT program and the money the city gets to run it."

"But wait, FDMA gives the city money to subsidize DERT. It shouldn't come out of the city funds, should it?"

Carol shook her head. "It's not enough, and the city is running out of money to pay the fire and police departments personnel. The FDMA can't pay the city personnel, so the city cuts back on the fire department and FDMA takes over the DERT and hands over the training program to the Dragon Logistics contractors."

"That's a horrible idea."

"Yes, it is. We'll need our own militia to combat the martial law they'd enact, it would be chaos."

"But then Dragon would have to actually move onto the island. If a major earthquake happened, we'd be cut off from the mainland. No bridges, no tunnels."

"Exactly. Marshal Law. Do you think military contractors, I mean emergency services contractors, are going to care about the elder facilities on the island? They just need a toe hold on our island, then after that they can do what they want." Carol shook her head and grimaced.

"Wow, I didn't know all that. How'd you find that out?" Annie asked.

"Who do you think lives in nursing facilities?"

"The elderly and infirmed."

"And they have children – who work for the city."

"Oh, right." Annie put her head back down and dug into her salad.

Lorna walked onto the Featherstone's front porch delicately. The wood beneath her feet looked rotten. She pushed the doorbell but didn't hear a chime. She couldn't keep her eyes off her feet. She really should not be standing on this rotting wood. She knocked hard and fast and took a few steps backwards off the front porch and stood on the top stair and waited.

"Hi ya."

Lorna whirled around and saw Running Bear's toothy grin shinning at her. "Hi."

Running Bear was looking at her cast. "You're that woman from class."

"Yes, I'm Lorna."

"Right. What can I help you with?"

"I was going to ask you about the night I came into class, well, I was sort of in shock. And I knew where you lived - this is where Jimmy used to come a lot."

"Jimmy?"

"Yeah, my friend Jimmy. The one who's missing? No one has seen him all week."

"Is that why you came here? To find Jimmy? He's not here."

"Nope. He's not." Lorna had accomplished her goal of rattling Running Bear's chain. She flashed a demonic toothy smile back as she walked away.

Running Bear started to crack. "I don't know what anyone has told you but we don't know what happened to Jimmy."

Out from behind Running Bear, flitted Rose. Lorna drew imaginary tentacles on Roses head to complete her butterfly outfit. "Hello! I'm so glad to see you up and about!" With a great flap of her yellow wing she cooed, "Come on back to the garden."

Lorna followed them, ducking through the overgrown walkway to the weedy, detritus strewn back yard.

"Please have a seat." Rose took a seat on a giant redwood stump and Lorna followed suit on another stump. Running Bear went inside.

Rose continued, "We could hear you through the kitchenette door in the classroom facility. I felt so bad for you. It must have been awful. You're not thinking of leaving DERT now are you? Is there anything we can do to help you? Can I get you something to drink? Homemade wine maybe?"

Lorna sat back and took in Rose's performance. These two are fucking weird. "No thanks, I really just stopped by to see if anyone found my cell phone."

Running Bear came back outside with a large bottle and three glasses.

"Really, thank you, but I'm on antibiotics."

Running Bear shook his head. "Antibiotics will kill you."

Lorna did a double take. "Well don't tell that to amputees. You know people used to die from strep-throat before penicillin."

"I'm not talking about penicillin. I'm talking about all those damn derivatives and synthetics they've got now a-days – don't let your body make its own immune system."

Lorna nodded but said, "I'll take my chances."

Running Bear exhaled loudly through his nose and lifted his lower lip over his moustache. "What's wrong with you?"

Lorna looked up at the passing clouds above. She unwrapped the gauze above her cast and showed them the cuts around her forearm.

"Good Lord!" Rose grabbed her chest.

Running Bear nodded knowingly. "Cops did that didn't they? Bastards."

"Yeah." Lorna said truculently.

Running Bear stood up. "Stay there, I've got some ointment I make for that."

Lorna started to say no, but he moved too quickly back inside.

Rose leaned in conspiratorially. "He makes it from aloe and lavender." She cut her eyes lower and whispered, "And something else. He won't tell me."

"It's not poop is it?"

Rose leaned back and took a beat before guffawing loudly and slapping Lorna on the back. Lorna winced at the sharp pain in her shoulder.

Suddenly Rose stopped laughing and said with mock sincerity, "Could be." Then delighted herself with another whooping guffaw that ended with a snort. "Oh I do love young people. People our age, ya' know, no sense of humor in 'em."

Running Bear came back outside carrying an old jelly jar filled with clear goo.

"Keep it lubricated with this so it won't scar and it'll heal faster." He said. "It smells pretty too." He opened the jar and held it out for her to smell.

Lorna leaned down and took a whiff. It did smell nice. "Well thank you. Can I like pay you for this or something?"

Simultaneously Rose and Running Bear were taken aback. "Absolutely not!" "Your money is no good!" "No! Huh uh." "You will not!"

"I'm sorry, I didn't mean to insult you." Lorna was caught off guard.

"No, it's just the right thing to do. You see. we help." Rose explained with long vowels in her words.

"Okay." Lorna looked around for an escape route. Rose was beginning to give her the hebe-gebee's and she smelled a little like cat pee and mothballs. Lorna unscrewed the cap again and took a deep whiff. "It is lovely. Thank you."

"You're welcome Lorna. And if those cops give you a hard time again, you let us know. We know people."

Lorna nodded.

"I don't want to pry and it's okay not to say, but what were you arrested for?" Rose asked.

"Oh it's okay, I was arrested by a man named Jenkins for trespassing, vandalism, and assault." Lorna stopped and started again, "And maybe some other stuff. See I came out of the hangar where I was listening to my radio and I ran into a security guard. I got into an altercation and that's how *this* happened," Lorna held up her cast. "The next day this Jenkins shows up and arrests me for listening to my radio in the hangar and assaulting the security guard. And *that* is how I got these." Lorna left out the part about Jimmy on purpose.

"But you said you found a body." Rose asked.

"I fell on it."

Rose gasped. Running Bear braced himself. "Was it Jimmy?"

Lorna paused a moment for full effect. "Yes, I think it was."

Rose gasped again and scurried inside.

"Do you know why Jimmy would be there?" Lorna asked.

Running Bear shook his head. His face flushed and quickly lost its pallor.

"Because someone moved his body after I left. When the cops went back they didn't find it. So now, of course, they think I'm a crazy hysteric."

Lorna waited for Running Bear's reaction but he was definitely thinking about something.

"What did you see?" Running Bear finally asked. "I mean, how was he killed?"

"I don't know. I identified him from a high school picture Mrs. Strangler had."

"Well, I don't understand. Did he have anything with him? Was he laid there, like did someone put him there or is that where he died?"

"I'm so sorry. I don't know."

Lorna had heard enough from the Featherstones and stood up. "Thank you for the ointment Running Bear. I guess I'll see you tonight." He didn't even ask why she had said she was looking for Jimmy when she first arrived.

Running Bear nodded. "Thank you Lorna. Thank you for letting us know."

"You're welcome."

Detective Keeling was deeply reluctant to have a conversation with the fire department's Battalion Chief Jules about a problem within the police department. But the only way to find out just how deep in Dragon Logistics pockets anyone from the police department could be, is through Jules and DERT. He believed Jules had the ear, not just of the city council, but also FDMA and God knows who else.

Roberta popped her head into his office, "Lunch." It wasn't a request.

Keeling stood up, threw on his blue blazer and followed Roberta out.

"It's a little early for lunch isn't it?" He asked catching up with her on the sidewalk.

"I'm not hungry. I'm going over to have a conversation with Pullam and see what he knows about anyone using a cell phone after we left the class."

"I need you to have one with the security guard who fought with Lorna though."

"I already did. I told him I was following up an inquiry about her arrest. It's only a matter of time before that gets back to Jenkins."

"Right. I'll tell him I sent you. What'd he say?"

"Same thing that was on the complaint, verbatim. I asked about the gun she claimed he had and he denied it. He was nervous. Said he did not go into the hangar after the scuffle but ran after her and just went back to his truck."

"Didn't say *how* he knew who she was?"

"Nope. What'd you find out about Jenkins?"

Keeling shook his head. "Nothing. He's a few years out from retirement, he may be looking to line his coffers though."

They stopped walking in front of the fire department administrative offices. "Want to come along?" Roberta asked flicking her head toward the offices.

"No, I'll slip in here for a slice. Come by and get me when you're finished."

Keeling stepped into the Slice is Nice pizza parlor as Roberta continued on to the fire department offices.

Captain Pullam looked up at Roberta as she strode into his office. "You know I was wondering if you guys would come by or not."

Roberta took the seat offered her across from his desk, "It's just routine. So what happened after we left?"

"We just regrouped and went on with the search and rescue lecture. We talked about safety and proper equipment. Oh and we went over cribbing."

"Do you recall anyone using a cell phone? Did anyone make any phone calls?"

"Yes, several people. Okay, after you guys left I asked them to take a break. One guy Craig used the bathroom and his buddy Ryan pulled out his phone. Let me think," Pullam lowered his head and closed his eyes in thought. "John Wu called his wife I think because Christopher got on the phone. I was arranging the handouts for the cribbing and looked over and Charley and that other guy were talking and Carol - yeah I don't know, but I thought Mrs. Strangler had left as well but she came back in."

Roberta lifted her eyebrows. "Wow, that's pretty good."

Pullam smiled. "Ginkgo, I take it every morning."

"What is that?"

"A mineral supplement or a maybe a vitamin, helps with memory."

"So, no one else has been by to ask you about the state of mind Lorna was in when she arrived?"

"No, I mean you were there, with Detective Keeling." Pullam broke off, he paused before he crossed his arms over his chest, leaned forward and said softly, "What's going on?"

Roberta pressed her lips together and shook her head slowly.

"Above your pay grade? Me too. But if you ever want to exchange notes be sure to come back by. I think we could have a very receptive and productive conversation, for Keeling too, of course. I think both of our bosses would see eye to eye. Especially when it comes to ridding the island of *rats*." Pullam nodded and leaned back.

Roberta stood up. "Well, thanks for the chat. Ginkgo, I'll have to try it."

Roberta showed herself out the way she came in and casually walked down the street into the pizza parlor. Keeling was finishing his slice and slid the paper plate holding a second slice toward Roberta. Roberta took the empty cup that sat on the table to the soda fountain and poured herself a soda before sitting down.

"Well," she smiled, "thanks for the lunch."

Keeling smiled back. "What?"

"Unless I'm deeply mistaken, I believe you have a couple of friends eager to talk with you over at the fire station."

"About what? What do you mean?"

"Pullam said if you ever want to exchange notes that you and his boss, no, he said it would be a productive and receptive conversation and that our bosses, you and Jules would see eye to eye about ridding the island of rats."

"About what?"

"He said, rats. But I think it has something more to do with the DERT program and Dragon Logistics. I'm guessing they are looking for more backing to oppose the take over."

Keeling shook his head. "One thing at a time."

Roberta swallowed a bite of pizza and shrugged, "Can't hurt. Aren't you always talking about alliances?"

Keeling grimaced. "Am I?"

Roberta nodded, chewing another bite.

Roberta's radio sprung to life and Keeling's beeper went off at the same time. They both grabbed their devices and looked at them before looking back up and shaking their heads to one another.

Captain Pullam rushed into Chief Jules office. "Got a minute?"

"Several." Jules pulled his legs off his desk and slammed down a thick catalogue. "Did you see this?"

M. Saylor Billings

Captain Pullam leaned over the desk to look at the catalogue, the Dragon logo told him immediately it was not a catalogue. "What is that?"

"It's Dragon Logistics Incident Management Manual." Jules face was red and blotchy with rage.

"I have good news then. I just got a visit from a Sergeant Fitzgerald."

"Who's that?"

"She and Keeling were there that night but she came back to ask me if anyone had made any phone calls after they had left. When I pressed her about it she went silent, so I told her that our bosses might have common interests. Then she practically skipped out of the office."

Jules looked up at the ceiling. "Why would a Sergeant and a Detective come to DERT training class the same week Rick Kansas from FDMA and Dragon Logistics make their move?" Jules shook his head. "Before we play into the police department's agenda, let's make sure they can work with ours. Maybe I should drop in tonight, show my support for them, before Dragon takes over."

"I think that would be a good idea—"

The Fire alarm rang and Chief Jules moved his bulky frame like a ballet dancer around the office, grabbing his hat and pulling his black fire resistant coat on. Captain Pullam turned and strode back down the hall to his office.

Jimmy Marsh's body was bloated and discolored. Around his neck hung a cord that was connected to some type of radio. Roberta turned away momentarily, inhaled the sea air, and looked toward the horizon to regain her balance.

"Is that who I think it is?" Keeling asked.

"I think so, as far as I can tell at least."

The two walked back to their squad cars as the fire department busied themselves with the body bag.

"Well, I guess we have a homicide case. And that is *my* department." Keeling rocked forward.

"*You* have a homicide case Detective Keeling. I'm just a shift runner, I don't think the Captain—"

"I've been talking to the Captain about your work Sergeant." Keeling suddenly spoke in an official tone. "He wants to speak with you about your future with the department. I believe that conversation should happen sooner than later as I'd bet there is going to be an opening soon."

Roberta raised her eyebrows. "Why can't you just speak English?"

Keeling smiled wider than she'd ever seen him smile. "Okay bitch, get you're ass over to the brass, I put your name in for a promotion with the Captain!"

Roberta could not suppress it and burst out laughing. "You are just wrong. You know that? Your brain got a short circuit?"

"I was going to tell you at lunch but," he waved back at the body behind them.

Roberta nodded. "But when did you even have time to do that?"

"Yeah, well, y' know, but look, go over there when you can – tonight before the DERT class maybe. Before he leaves for the day. Just pop in, tell him I spoke with you and that you have a great interest in staying with the department and moving up. That's all you have to say. Don't make excuses or do anything else. Just go in state your case and move on. He likes that. You've earned this."

"Okay." Roberta was overwhelmed.

A large red SUV rolled to a stop next to Roberta's police cruiser, Chief Jules rolled down his window. "Good news?"

"No Chief, we have a body washed up, we're working on the I.D. now." Keeling said.

Jules turned his gaze toward Roberta. "Sergeant Fitzgerald, right?"

"Yes." Roberta stepped forward.

Jules nodded. "Good to meet you, finally, I've heard good things from my Captain." Jules turned back to Keeling. "I'm going to the DERT class tonight, to show my appreciation. How about a drink afterward?"

"Yeah," Keeling scratched his chin, "that'd be great. See you there."

Jules rolled his SUV forward and parked behind the fire truck.

Keeling turned back to Roberta. "Okay. So look, we need to get a positive ID so I'm going to try and find the next of kin."

"Oh. Hang on, the parents moved. Mrs. Strangler mentioned it. Damn, where was it?" Roberta said slowly, "She said they moved to...Clear Lake. They're in Clear Lake."

"Okay, Marsh in Clear Lake. Apropos, considering the situation." Detective Keeling moved toward his unmarked squad car, "Talk to the coroner - and don't forget the Captain."

"Thanks." Roberta climbed into her squad car and watched the ambulance leave.

"Mrs. Strangler, I know you're hurting, you really don't need to be here, we'll be glad—" Lorna said.

"I'm not hurting as much as you'll be if you don't stop coddling me."

Sally bit her lower lip to suppress a grin. Annie gave Lorna the no-no sign and tsk-tsked her. Just before they had arrived at Sally and Lorna's house, Annie and Mrs. Strangler had had a visit from Sergeant Fitzgerald with the news about finding Jimmy's body in the estuary.

The three women sat in Sally and Lorna's living room and exchanged their stories of the day. Mrs. Strangler told of Wyatt's visit and Charley's job with Carol and how Carol was starting a DERT program for the island nursing homes. "I've known Wyatt since he was a teenager and he was very unsettled about Jimmy missing but I'm just not sure if he was being completely forthright about that job he and Charley had with Dragon Logistics."

Annie nodded. "Carol mentioned the Dragon Logistics too."

"Dragon Logistics? Why does that name keep popping up? They're like military contractors, I don't understand what they'd have to do with this." Sally asked.

"We'll have to find out more from Roberta." Annie told her.

Lorna told of her visit to the Featherstones. "It was almost as if they were waiting for me. And Running Bear said, 'I don't know what happened to Jimmy', not 'We don't know where he is or Jimmy just stopped coming over'. He seemed truly devastated by the news of Jimmy but then he also asked if Jimmy had anything with him. Which I thought was weird. I think he was trying to nudge around to see if I thought Jimmy had this missing file or something. Which begs the question, why would Running Bear know about the file. I think you may be right Mrs. Strangler, they definitely know *something*."

"That's the same thing that cop asked you, right?" Mrs. Strangler asked.

"Yes. I think we have to assume it's the same thing."

Finally Annie spoke. "Mrs. Strangler what is wrong with that Judy?"

Mrs. Strangler shrugged, "I guess that's what happens to kids with such domineering Mothers."

"But she's not a kid, she's got to be at least forty years old."

Mrs. Strangler held out her hands, palms up, and shrugged again.

Annie continued, "Anyway, it does seem like Carol knows a lot about that Dragon Logistics. It all had to do with money from FDMA. I just didn't get a feeling it had anything to do with Jimmy."

Sally piped up, "Well did you think the two were connected?"

"Well yeah, why else would Jimmy have been in the DERT hangar to begin with?" Lorna said. "Something's missing, I just can't put my finger on it. Like there is a step missing or something. Y' know?" Lorna directed the question at Sally.

"You think he, what? He confronted them or was spying on them or something?"

Mrs. Strangler spoke, "No, they didn't have that drill for the city council until after Jimmy was missing."

"What if he was meeting someone there and they, you know, pushed him in the pit?" Sally said.

"The only way we're going to find out what happened is to find out who moved Jimmy's body. And the only way we can do that is if the police get some kind of forensic evidence, an eye witness, or somebody squawks about it." Lorna said with finality.

"We should go, maybe John Wu or those two other guys remember anything." Annie said getting up.

"What are you doing tonight?" Lorna turned to Sally.

"It's Friday night, I'm going to a bar maybe pick up some fast women." Sally smiled.

"Oh you're so coy. Just make sure they do windows before you seduce them with your vast intellect."

"I will." Sally puckered up and Lorna kissed her goodbye.

In the car Mrs. Strangler turned around in her seat and addressed Lorna. "Can I ask you something?"

"Sure."

"What do you see in her that you don't see in a man? Were you abused or something?"

"No. I dated men, a long time ago. Several really nice guys and, as a matter of fact, several jerks too. But, have you accidentally ever put the left shoe on your right foot? It's like that. Then one day, I had an 'Ah Ha' experience and I put my shoes on the right feet. It was a huge relief and everything in my life finally made sense. I mean I can't speak for all homosexuals but for me that's how I'd explain it."

Annie perked up and gleaned a look at Lorna in the rearview mirror. "So, Sally's a shoe?"

Lorna smiled. "You have to take care of your feet, they carry you everywhere."

Mrs. Strangler nodded in understanding. "So it's not the sex of the person that guides you but the right person, despite their sex."

"For me, yes, I guess you could say that. But I guess you could also say some women just really like to – "

"Lorna!" Annie cut her off.

"There's a lid for every pot, my Ma used to say," Mrs. Strangler said.

Annie laughed. "Wait then I believe you've had a couple of lids."

"I never said she was right."

CHAPTER 10

SALLY'S NEW FRIEND

An uncomfortable pall hovered over the classroom occupants. Lorna watched Craig and Ryan walk into the classroom, sit down, and pull out the white DERT binders from their backpacks.

Lorna saddled up to their table and reintroduced herself to Craig and Ryan. "Hi. I'm Lorna."

"Hi," each guy answered.

"How's your hand?" Craig asked.

Lorna held it up. "It throbs."

Ryan lifted her arm up to his eye level to look straight into it. "It's going to throb normally, but I think you might want to see the doctor if the throbbing gets too much for you, I'd hate for you to be having a circulation problem. That'd be bad."

"How do you know so much about this?" Lorna asked.

Ryan held up both hands to her revealing several crooked fingers. "Volleyball."

Lorna smiled. "Setter?"

167

Ryan made a triangle with his hands above his head and pushed up making a popping sound with his tongue.

Craig leaned in and lowered his voice. "So what really happened over there?"

"Car door." Lorna said and winked. She crouched down in front of them and lowered her voice, "After I left, did either one of you see someone use their cell phone?"

"I did. I called my voicemail," Ryan said.

Craig shrugged. "No, I don't know. I went to the bathroom. Sorry."

"Well, wait. John used his too, but I don't know it might have been Christopher," Ryan added.

Lorna rose back up. "Yeah, that's what I thought." She looked over to Annie who was in a conversation with Roberta and Christopher. The boy was pointing to things on Roberta's belt and she was explaining the various police paraphernalia she carried.

"Are you going to be able to do the drill with us?" Craig asked.

"Of course," Lorna said taking a step away. "Thanks for the advice."

Captain Pullam came in carrying two large boxes. Behind him, Chief Jules hoisted a giant canvas bag over his shoulder, looking not unlike Santa Clause in his red windbreaker, black fire boots, and three day old white facial stubble. Lorna's mouth fell open – *the greatest earthly incarnation of goodwill known to mankind. The universal symbol of that which could bring about the kindest actions in the most evil of hearts stood before her.* A chill ran up her spine and she wanted to scream. *He had come back for her.*

Annie saw Pullam first, then Jules, then Lorna. "Oh no," she gasped.

Roberta caught Annie's gaze and looked over to Lorna who was perfectly erect in her seat, smiling ear to

M. Saylor Billings

ear, her chest heaving. "What's wrong with her?" Roberta asked.

"You remember how women used to faint at the sight of Elvis? Santa is Lorna's Elvis."

Roberta looked over to Jules dropping the great canvas bag onto the floor in the front of the classroom. "Oh no."

Chief Jules straightened up and leaned over, stretching his back and barking out a long 'ohhhh.' To Lorna's ears, she had heard him bark a long 'ho ho ho', and she gave a soft clapping - hand to elbow - catching his attention. He gave a quick wave and cocked his head to the side in a questioning acknowledgement as he approached her. Annie stood frozen watching. If she moved too quickly, she might startle Lorna, but if she didn't move at all, they might carry Lorna away in a straight-jacket.

"Don't I know you?" Jules asked.

Lorna nodded.

"I'm Battalion Chief Jules, but everyone calls me Julie."

"Okay. I'm Lorna Tollison. I grew up in Atlanta, but I live here now, on Saint Charles Place. The big yellow house."

"Oh right, yeah. I know the place - across from Pink Senior Center. What happened to your hand?"

Lorna lied. "Car door." She couldn't very well tell him she had been in a fight. Just in case.

"You all right?"

"I am now, thank you."

"Didn't I see you the other day? You were looking for radio signals, right?"

"Yes. Yes, that was me. I saw you too. It was the highlight of my day."

Annie had slowly approached Lorna and slid down next to her.

Chief Jules stuck his wide hand out to her. "Chief Jules. Call me Julie."

"I'm Annie. It's nice to meet you."

Lorna added, "She lives on Saint Charles Place too, but across Liberty Avenue from me. 68 Saint Charles Place."

Julie nodded. "Yep, I know that one too. Craftsman Bungalows along that block."

"Yes. Wow, that's good." Annie smiled.

"Been doing this a long time," Julie said. "Excuse me, I'd like to meet the others."

"Thank you for stopping by," Annie said as Lorna appeared across the tabletop next to Julie.

Lorna hugged him. "Thank you."

Julie turned to meet Christopher, who was sitting wide eyed with his knees in the chair, his mouth agape. Lorna remained standing too close to Julie.

"Lorna, Roberta needs you outside. Lorna. Lorna."

"*What?*" Lorna shot back at Annie.

"Roberta, outside. *Now.*"

Sally cut the headlights off and parked the car outside the hangar door. She got out leaving the driver's side door unlocked. From across the yards and parking lots, she could see lights shining over at the Red Cross and DERT training class facilities. She opened the hangar door to make it appear that she had gone inside, then walked far enough away that she could see the car and hangar door but still stay out of the lamplights.

She toyed with the pipe wrench in her hands and waited. Finally, she saw the small security truck come to a stop and the headlights cut out. As she heard the engine cut off, she began casually walking back towards the hangar, careful to stay out of the streetlamps glow.

Focusing hard to make sure he matched Lorna's description of the guard, she planned her attack. He was a medium sized man and she knew her only chance to exploit the situation was the element of surprise. The guard opened the driver's side door and bent down inside. Sally reached over, unlatched his gun from its holster, and tossed the gun to the side. The guard struggled back out of the car, but Sally cracked him on the back of the head with the pipe wrench and pulled him onto the ground. Slamming the door shut, she sat on his back. He began to struggle again so she gave him another whack and leaned down with all her weight on his shoulder blades.

"Listen! Do I have your attention?" she growled in his ear.

The security guard moved his head.

"Now, I know you are just doing your job out here. But I'm going to kill you with your own gun in that hangar unless you tell me what I want to hear. Do you understand that?"

The security guard nodded.

"Good. You remember that woman you beat up? I'm her partner. Wasn't that nice of me? I just told you exactly who I am, saving you a lot of trouble. Right?"

He nodded again.

"Right. Now then, you are going to tell me who you are working for and who moved that body out of here the other night. And I'm going to make sure that no one knows it was you who told me. That way, you can keep your job here and my partner doesn't have to worry about false arrests anymore. Got that?" Sally dug her knee deeper into the back of his neck and pulled his head up by his hair. "What?"

He gave a choking grunt and struggled to nod again and she released his head.

"Jenkins. Jenkins moved the body. I don't know who killed him. I called Jenkins because I saw her come out and I just was going to ask her what she was doing but she was so freaked out. Then she kicked me. I didn't mean to break her hand I was just defending myself. Please. She was crazy."

"And?"

"And what?"

"Why Jenkins?"

"He helped me get this job. He told to me to call him first if anything happens here on the base. He's my first call. Then I call a patrol car if I have any problems. A few nights before – that night before the earthquake – he told me to keep people away from this hangar because of that drill Dragon was running. But then after she attacked me I could hear something, I thought someone else was in the hangar. Then when I got back I saw it was a radio and that body. So I called Jenkins. And we got it out of the pit and he took it away."

"How?"

"Um, I don't know what you mean. The back seat of his car?"

"That's good. What's your name?"

"Please."

Sally grabbed his hair and pulled up.

"I'm Kevin. Kevin Lawrence."

"Okay, Kevin. Now we know each other. Do me a favor. Get rid of that stupid gun. Twice now it's almost gotten you killed. I don't like it when my friends get killed, you understand?"

"Yes."

"I'm going to let you up now. No one has to know we've met, but if you do something stupid and I hurt you, you're going to have a lot of explaining to do - got that?"

"Yes."

Sally climbed off his back and stood up. Kevin leaned up on all fours and held the pose of a minute, waiting for his strength to recover.

"You're blocking my car door Kevin. You have to get up and get some ice for your head."

"Okay." Kevin stood up and took a couple of shaky steps.

She suppressed the urge to reach out and bash Kevin in the head again by taking a step back away from him. A twinge of guilt shot through Sally. She realized the adrenaline was wrecking havoc on her nervous system. She slowly inhaled and exhaled. She got back into the car and slowly drove away.

A highly perturbed Lorna stomped out to find Roberta leaning into Keeling's squad car. "*What*?" she demanded truculently.

Lorna caught Roberta and Keeling off guard. Keeling looked to Roberta in surprise.

"I was just telling Keeling about your meeting with the Featherstones today."

"So? I was talking to *Julie*."

"Yeah, I have a meeting with him later tonight," Keeling said.

Lorna facial muscles tightened. "You do? Are you going to talk about me?"

"Did you want me to?"

"Only if you're going to tell him I've been good this year."

Is she playing me? Keeling thought, but said, "Of course."

"Let me ask you something," Roberta said. "Did you go into their house?"

"The Featherstones? No."

"Turns out, those two have a pretty long sheet," Keeling said. "Especially 'Running Bear' Featherstone. Also known as Ronald Rosenbaum."

"Rosenbaum?" Lorna asked.

"They took the wife's last name, which helps mask his identity as well."

"Well, also, she would have been Rose Rosenbaum. Can't blame that," Lorna offered. "Did you find out any more about that idiot who arrested me? 'Cause you know he's on *someone's* payroll."

Keeling looked at Roberta and back at Lorna. "You've got a criminal mind. You know that?"

"Well, it just makes sense. He was trying to scare me off. Off of what? These people," Lorna nodded at the classroom, "didn't have anything to do with what happened to Jimmy. It has to do with that file he was asking me about. Find the file and you found the murderer."

"Don't be so sure of yourself. The absence of evidence or a phone call does not prove innocence," Roberta said.

"What?" Keeling asked, he had never heard such a preposterous –

"You heard me," Roberta snapped. "And we don't know it was murder yet."

Keeling asked Lorna, changing the subject, "How's Mrs. Strangler doing?"

"She's sad," Lorna said, eyes not moving off of Roberta. "She's taking the night off. She thinks it was the Featherstones too, but it doesn't make sense."

Keeling sighed. "Well, the coroner can't get to the body for a couple of days, but from the initial look she thought that angle of the wound made it seem like it was self-inflicted. Meaning, he fell into that pit. Which gives us a whole new set of why, how, and what for's."

The scabs on Lorna's wrists were beginning to itch. She rubbed them in thought. "Hmm, I don't know but it seems to me that–it's just so easy to think that everything is somehow connected. When it's not we look for links or ways to fit circles into squares. I think it's all about me 'cause I'm in my circle, but of course it's not about me. I mean that's what's really happening here – it's linear, but made to look like circles." She swirled around her right hand at the stars above. "I mean it just might be a series of events that aren't connected.

Most murders are committed because of passion – passion for money, love, or just insanity. So it's someone close to them. Right?"

Keeling and Roberta nodded.

"But if he fell and died, and someone moved the body, then they were covering up for a completely separate crime. Either that or you're looking for a lunatic."

Finally Keeling said, "Well, that's one way to look at it."

"Fine, okay well, is that all?" Lorna asked.

"Uh, sure. Thanks for the insight," Keeling said.

"Don't forget to give me props with," Lorna jerked her thumb toward the facility, "*you know who.*"

"Will do."

Roberta watched Lorna enter the building, shaking her head. "Sometimes I think she's on the other side of the glass looking in. Y'know?"

Keeling pulled the edges of his mouth down and nodded. "Okay I'll see you later. I've got a couple of stops to make." Keeling started the car engine. "Do you know what they're doing after this?"

"Annie said her husband was due back tonight so I imagine they'll just head home. Tomorrow is their big drill."

"I'm so glad to finally meet you in person. This is my daughter Judy."

Chief Jules looked down at Judy and smiled. Judy's face was unchanged so he didn't offer his hand but nodded. "It's good to meet you both."

"Not tonight, of course, but I was wondering if I could meet with you again, say, in about a week. I'd like to get your input on a proposal I'm assembling for a DERT type program for the nursing facilities on the island. I've gathered the other island nursing facilities directors and have made a preliminary outline." Carol pulled out a small red binder.

"That's a wonderful idea. I think Pullam – where is he?" Jules looked around and saw Pullam assembling the paperwork and backpacks together. "I think that's great and I'd be happy to meet with you anytime but the person you really need to talk to is Pullam. But yes, I think that is a great idea. Good job."

Lorna took her seat again next to Annie who was talking with Wyatt.

"I'm so sorry Wyatt. His parents came down from Clear Lake and I believe they are at Mrs. Strangler's now. But I'm sure they wouldn't mind you stopping by, but maybe tomorrow. I mean, I'd call ahead first."

"Well, thank you. I will." Stone faced, Wyatt strode back over to his seat next to Charley.

"Dude," Lorna said watching Wyatt.

"I know."

Charley slid the thin red binder he was thumbing through over to Wyatt who moved it back. Charley put the binder back in front of Wyatt, pointed to it, and looked around the room. Lorna smiled at him and he jerked his head back to the front of the room, leaned over and whispered to Wyatt. Wyatt was looking at the binder and shook his head in response.

"What do you think they're talking about?" Lorna asked.

"Who?" Annie asked.

"Wyatt and Charley. You just told Wyatt about Jimmy, didn't you?"

"Yes, poor guy."

"But he's not telling Charley."

"So? Pullam is about to announce it to the whole class."

"I wish we could see everyone's reactions when he does."

"Okay!" Captain Pullam began the class. "We've got a lot to go over tonight. But first I have some sad news. As you well know, our classmate Jimmy Marsh went missing after the Red Cross section of the program. Well, Jimmy's body washed ashore today."

The room went silent. Lorna scanned the back of heads and saw Rose bend down. Running Bear comforted his wife. Annie's eyes were on Wyatt and Charley. Upon hearing the news, Charley turned to Wyatt who stared straight ahead.

"Who is that?" Christopher said loudly and wanted to know from his father. "What happened?"

John Wu stood up, muttering, "We'll be right back," and took his son outside. Chief Jules accompanied the two out through the kitchenette. Craig pulled off his spectacles and looked around the room making eye contact with Lorna. Annie noticed Carol reaching her arm over Judy's shoulder.

"So," Pullam continued, "I've not heard from Mrs. Strangler. Annie do you know if she'll be with us tomorrow?"

"No Captain, I don't know yet, but I'll try to find out and let you know?"

"That'd be great. If you'll extend our condolences in the meantime? And I think it would be appropriate if we begin tomorrow's drill with a moment of silence in Jimmy's honor?"

People mumbled their agreement.

"Okay, next. Now, tomorrow's drill is going to be a bit different from our usual graduation and orientation drill. You will still graduate and be oriented into section 8. And other DERT members will be playing the victims and survivors for us. However, due to budgetary cuts and some type of FDMA handout to Dragon Emergency Management, the DERT training and the disaster services for the island will now be under their watchful eyes. So I don't actually know exactly what this means for the DERT volunteers right now."

"What are you saying?" Lorna wanted to know.

"Just what I said," Captain Pullam said. "Dragon Emergency Management is taking over the DERT program and the disaster services for the island."

John Wu and Christopher came in took their seats again. Ryan looked over to Christopher and gave him a sympathetic smile. Christopher turned away from him and stared ahead.

Craig raised his hand. "How can a for profit company take over a non-profit with volunteers?"

Pullam raised his eyebrows and inhaled loudly. "Good question. The representatives from the company will be with us tomorrow, I believe they'll start their marketing campaign to you then, it's my understanding that they have big plans for the program."

"What *big plans*?" Running Bear said in disgust. "Those types of companies are in *business*. Businesses make money. This program is a community volunteer program. We don't make money."

Rose jumped up from her seat. "We're here for each other in crisis, not for a company who makes money in crisis. Do you have any idea the kinds of bills these people can stick this island for?"

"Okay," Pullam held his hands up in surrender. "I totally agree with you. But look, this came down from the city council."

Rose began gathering her coat and binder up.

"Wait! Please Mrs. Featherstone, don't leave -hear me out. Please."

Rose jammed her hand onto her hip and cocked her head sideways at him.

"Now, let's say we all – volunteers and cops and firemen – everyone who makes up the program just said 'To heck with this' and we all quit DERT. Right? We leave the program. But that's just what Dragon would want. That way they could sock us with some type of outrageous bill - they would need to hire more people, more facilities, more equipment, and, you're right, we'd pay for it. But if we stay, then we'd staff it and at least have a voice."

"This is crazy. I've never heard of such a thing," Ryan said aloud. "They could in effect impose martial law if there was a disaster here."

"Would that be such a bad thing?" John Wu asked.

Ryan turned on John. "Duh! Katrina?"

"Oh please," John answered in disgust.

Craig turned around. "Why not? If they are sanctioned by FDMA, which is the federal government, they absolutely could."

"Whoa, let's not get ahead of ourselves," Pullam pleaded. "How about this - how about we go through our drill tomorrow and afterward we'll talk again. We'll hear them out and regroup. Is that okay? I mean, what if it simply comes down to them wanting to fill in the gaps? Providing evacuation services, emergency medical and just transportation."

"I still don't like it," Running Bear grumbled aloud.

"Fair enough, but come on, you've all worked so hard in the past two weeks. Let's not just throw it away. Okay?"

Annie and Lorna turned to Roberta who sat in the corner giving Pullam a goggle-eyed stare.

Lorna leaned over to Annie. "She looks exhausted."

Annie nodded as Pullam continued, "Okay, I want you guys to do well tomorrow." He smiled almost to himself and mumbled, "It's a point of pride for me." He held up a yellow backpack with the black DERT letters on it. "So first we're going to go over what's inside here, then we'll do a quick review of divisions. But first, what's the first three things to think about in a disaster?"

Everyone responded, "Safety. Safety. Safety."

"Who are the first three people you should care for?"

Everyone droned out loud together, "Ourselves, our family, our community."

"Why?"

"We can't help others if we are in need."

"Very good."

Lorna leaned over to Annie. "When did you say Tim was getting back?"

Annie held up eight fingers.

Lorna showed Annie her cell phone, which read: 7:13 PM.

Annie rolled her eyes and made a *gah* sound.

Mrs. Jules sat in her favorite chair in her parlor reading the newspaper when the phone rang.

"Hello?"

"Mother, it's Glynnis."

"Yes, dear."

"Well, I've got good news. The council accepted our circular and we've got 75 volunteers for tomorrow. I called a section leader from the DERT program and he's gathered the troops. Anyone not helping with the training drill is going to be out getting signatures for the recall and initiative."

"Oh that's wonderful. What a nice turnout. I think there we only need twenty five hundred signatures for the initiative. Now did you find out if Tam was tipped off?"

"Well, no, but I'm sure. You can't keep something like this a secret for too long."

"No. And we can't be seen to look like we're being sneaky."

"No, of course."

"Well done. Now tell me where I need to be tomorrow and what time."

Keeling rolled his Jeep next to The Lemon Suds Bar and looked around the parking lot. A small part of him was relieved to see the Battalion Chief had not used his city issued SUV for his private use. He went in to the dingy, darkened bar and saw the unmistakable white head of hair peaking out the top of the high backed booths.

"Nice place," he said to Jules.

Jules shrugged. "So, what's going on over there in the police department?"

This time Keeling shrugged. "Well, I've got a homicide on my hands that involves someone who was in the DERT program. *Which*," Keeling added quickly, "wouldn't mean anything special except someone else from the DERT program found it and then the body got dumped into the estuary. And that's a problem."

Jules emptied his glass and looked around the dim bar. "Look. I think you and I can help each other out, but first I need to know if it's mutually beneficial."

"Well, first of all, I think we've got some city people on someone else's payroll."

Jules nodded. "Delores Tam."

"Really?" Keeling was surprised and leaned forward. "I was talking about Jenkins from property crimes."

Jules quickly searched his memory for a 'Jenkins.'

"Heavy guy, balding, kinda—" Keeling squinted his eyes and pushed out his lips.

"Oh yeah, I think I've seen him a few times. He always shows up at house fires. Brown suit?"

"Yes. That's him."

"Well, he's not putting money into his wardrobe," Jules laughed. "I have the same types of problems in my battalion as well. So you need something on him to prove it?"

Keeling rubbed the stubble on his chin. "I think it's more than that. What do you know about this Dragon situation?"

"I think that it was completely orchestrated by Delores Tam and the city council. I talked to a buddy of mine on the council. He said he thinks someone from Dragon contacted her and she saw fit to convince the city council that giving them the DERT contract it was a sure way to save money on our pensions and man-hours. FDMA and Homeland Security has some extra cash to spend and instead of spending it on the state and cities, they're handing it out to their contractor buddies, like Dragon. But that's not our problem. The only way we're going to prove that Delores Tam is taking money is to contact the city attorney and have her officially investigated. To do that, someone is going to have to bring charges against her."

"Well that would explain why that body was dumped into the estuary," Keeling said and took another gulp of beer.

Julie nodded. "Tam doesn't want any bumps in the road for Dragon's transition of the DERT program. Nothing to get into the press and nothing to alert people so - "

"So maybe Lorna was right after all," Keeling smiled.

"Lorna? With the broken hand?"

"Yeah, she thinks you're Santa Claus."

Julie smiled.

"That's got to get old for you, Julie."

"Nope. I *love* it. I can't wait for my mustache to grow back. I always get a little depressed after I shave it, but my wife...." Julie mumbled off and shrugged.

"And it forces you to drink in places like this," Keeling smiled. "It's the seedy side of Santa."

Jules swallowed his gulp of beer ignoring Keeling's judgmental comment. "I've got a call in to Allen Wood, works with the city manager. I've been waiting to hear back from him. If there has been any hanky panky going on, he'll know about it. What is it I can do to help the investigation though?"

"Is there any way you could get to Delores Tam, pressure her somehow?"

Jules shook his head in disgust and drained his mug. "Well I don't want to be too obvious about it but I think I'll head down for the drill tomorrow. I'm sure Pullam will be glad to have the help. How about you?"

Keeling pulled out his wallet. "I don't want to make anyone suspicious yet. Now, I need to go see a man about a horse. What do I owe ya for the beer?"

Jules waved his hand. "Next time."

Keeling very much agreed with Julies sentiment. "Alright, thanks for the beer Julie." Keeling said as he walked out.

When someone called after them, Lorna and Annie walking to Annie's car. "Hang on a minute?"

They turned around to see Wyatt.

"I'm sorry to bother you. Should I go over there to see his parents? Tonight, I mean. I should say something."

"I'm sure that you mean well but I really don't think now is a good time at all," Annie said.

"I need to help. Maybe Mrs. Strangler needs an errand run."

Lorna spoke up. "Wyatt. Listen to me. Your wanting to help right now has more to do with your feelings than helping someone else. If you *must* go over, you should ask if you could bring something for them. Food, a couple boxes of tissue, aspirin, something that will help alleviate *their* needs. They just got the worst news parents can ever get."

"She's right, Wyatt. But maybe they'd have questions for you. I mean you guys hung out a lot recently with Charley. Right?"

"No. I mean up until a few weeks ago, sure. But, uh...." Wyatt broke off and seemed to remember something. "I need to go. Thanks."

"What about Mrs. Strangler?" Annie asked after him.

"I need to find Charley. I'll try to stop by."

Lorna and Annie got in the car. "What was that about?" Lorna asked.

"I don't know but I don't think it's good news."

Austin and Greg looked over the copy of the ransom note again. The note read: *$10,000 Friday. DERT drill. Have Dragon Logistics leave the bag in the hangar where you left your last package.*

Bill watched them patiently, making sure they took in his story completely. Bill kept the real ransom note in his wallet.

"What other package, sir?" Greg asked.

Bill raised his eyebrows innocently. "I have no idea. I'd guess it has something to do with the councilwoman. But look, I think I found the place that this note is referring to. In the hangar, behind their scaffolding, is an old oil-changing pit. Leave the moneybag in there. Greg, I've got your Saturday Special rigged up in this bag. Make sure the moment you light it, you get out quick. The whole point of this thing is to burn fast, so after Austin makes the drop and comes back to your position, the two of you make tracks out of there."

"Sir? Uh, if you know who sent this, I mean why not just give it to the police. Why burn the place down?"

"Not my choice. I'm under orders here. It's between the councilwoman and our bosses. I imagine they already have plans for that space that don't include a training hangar. This way, the insurance will take care of it for them, probably recoup some of the money they've spent."

"What about casualties?" Greg asked.

"With that many fireman and DERT members around? Won't happen. Plus with all the confusion, we can pin point who sent the note and pull them aside. You two okay with this assignment?"

"Yeah, absolutely," Greg said. Austin nodded his agreement.

"Austin?" Bill challenged Austin.

"Sir, yes sir. We can't have bribery."

"Good. Let's go through the movements again."

The Disaster Relief Club

CHAPTER 11

TIM AND MICHAEL ALLIANCE

Michael handed over his boarding pass to the ticket taker, a little disappointed that there was no first class on this airline, but not enough to ruin his day. He had other disappointments on his mind. From here on out he would lead a dual life. This was not how he had pictured his future. But now, he needed a story to tell his friends, his family, and his coworkers – who were now his former coworkers – about his new position in the FBI.

Michael took his seat next to an older woman with neatly cropped grey hair. She was already reading her book and did not look at him as he sat down and buckled his seatbelt.

Before Michael had left the farmhouse, Frank had put together a trade publication, entitled *Prohouse Insulation Manufacturing,* which contained most of what they had taught him. It was a study manual, and he thumbed through the "Financial Forecasting" section that contained notes on his cover operations in the Special Fraud Division and coded bank accounts. Clever,

Michael thought. Michael pulled out the second book that Elliot had given to him, *Robinson Crusoe* by Daniel Dafoe. Very apt, Michael nodded to himself. He leaned his chair back and closed his eyes – next stop, Phoenix.

Michael rolled his eyes at the row of American made sedans on the Perks car rental lot. Very ambiguous, he thought sarcastically. Randomly selecting a sedan, he drove to the hotel downtown, which turned out to be much closer to the airport than he thought.

He was hungry but, because of the time change he had a couple of hours before he imagined Tim would return to the hotel and the restaurant would be open. Michael took a shower, placed fresh dressing on his leg, and dressed in his suit. He went downstairs to grab a coffee, read his trade publication, and wait in the lobby. By seven o'clock, he was worried. There was no sign of Tim, so he went over to the lobby desk.

"Hi, I'm Michael Chan in room 312. I flew in today and was supposed to meet an associate, Tim Doughall, at 5:00 here in the lobby. He hasn't shown up and I'm worried about him."

"Okay," the receptionist nodded and looked at his trade publication.

"Well, did he leave a message for me? Is there anyway to check that?"

"Hang on. You checked into your in room today. Did you have a reservation?"

"No."

"Give me a minute. Let me go check any shift notes. We have a notebook in back."

The receptionist left the counter and Michael looked at the entrances and exits. Could Tim have walked out and I not seen him? he asked himself.

"There were no notes left in the reception notebook," the receptionist said.

"Do I have the right hotel?" Michael said aloud. "Can you check for me?"

The receptionist shook her head and stuttered out, "I don't know."

Michael realized she would not be able to give out guest information and said, "You probably can't check guest registration and tell me who's here..." and added quietly and slowly, "...but you could tell me if I have the right hotel in which to meet a business colleague and hold meetings. Because I could be in a lot of trouble if I've made a mistake, *a lot of trouble*."

The receptionist nodded and cleared her throat, covertly glancing around the lobby area. She made a few key stokes on the computer and shook her head without looking up at him. She continued shaking her head slowly and making eye contact while saying, "We do have a business center and meeting rooms if that would interest you."

Michael patted the counter. "Thank you, no. We can meet in the restaurant." He paused and added sincerely, "Thank you."

She gave him a pitiful smile as he walked away.

Michael didn't have time to check his carry-on at the airport and slid the case in the overhead compartment. How far behind Tim could he be? Michael's stomach growled as he plopped down next to a large balding guy crammed into the small seat with his business jacket folded in his lap.

Michael's stomach growled the whole two-hour flight to Oakland. After de-boarding, he headed straight for a fast food joint in the airport.

The circa 1980's Oldsmobile deal that had been left for him in long-term parking was a redwood color. Well, he thought, you wanted ambiguous, and tossed his carry on into the passenger seat.

He parked down the street from 68 Saint Charles Place and looked at the Tim's house. Nobody home, no lights on.

Walking around the block, he could see down a driveway that led to a wooden fence behind the house and divided the lots between Tim's backyard and the neighbors. Michael didn't hesitate. He casually walked up the driveway and lifted himself over the fence with purpose. But he split a couple of the sutures in his leg and winced hard when he landed on the other side. Light streamed from a crack in the basement window. He crouched down and looked at the black fabric that had been placed on the other side of the window. Dogs began to bark loudly from inside the house and the basement light went out. Michael stood up against the house and held his breath. The back sliding glass door opened and Tim stepped out on to the patio.

Michael stepped out of the shadow. "Funny, I didn't figure you as a backdoor guy."

Tim swung around and squinted. "I, didn't figure you as a," Tim paused, "a chink?"

Michael shrugged. "I prefer kuli. I'm Michael Chan from the FBI." Michael stuck out his hand for Tim.

"Tim Doughall."

"Is there somewhere we can talk?"

"Sure. Come inside." Tim turned and walked into the house. He flipped on a light in the kitchen that Michael immediately turned back off.

Tim swung back on him. "What are you doing?"

Michael went back outside to the patio and Tim followed.

"I don't think you are supposed to be home and I don't want to blow your cover," Michael said softly. "Are we *safe* here?"

Tim shook his head no.

"Your handler was killed the other day and I'm his replacement."

"I know."

"How?"

"The boat blast – that was Rudolph's boat. I read about it."

"Rudolph?" Michael laughed. "Sorry."

"I knew that wasn't his real name."

"Of course. He was just a real character, that guy."

Tim did not share Michael's humor and stared at him.

"Look, we have to talk. Is there somewhere we can go?"

"I think the basement is okay." Tim said and led the way to the stairs inside.

They descended a rickety flight of stairs and into a musty basement where Tim flipped on a work light. Michael looked around at the workbench filled with old style electronics and various tools.

"What is this?" Michael asked.

"My workshop. I've been restoring old analogue pieces – radios, sonar trackers. I've been taking the digital technology and doing small workarounds. Like with this piece, it's a passive sonar—"

Michael stopped him. "Okay, that's great. But I need to go back a bit. We need to talk about Spectorgies. I need to know where you are, what objectives *Rudolph* gave you. My bosses are worried with his death. He may have put you in a bad position with the company."

Tim shook his head. "I don't understand - what objectives?"

Michael looked around the workshop. "Tim, what was your relationship with *Rudolph*?"

Tim blinked several times, paused a beat, and blinked again before saying, "He was great to me. Showed me his radio collection, y'know, we were buds." Tim resumed his blinking.

It suddenly dawned on Michael that Tim was sending him Morris code.

"Oh right. So he never spoke to you about any company secrets or tried to get you to reveal anything that could result in his death? We have to check all the angles of a possible murder. Did he share anything he was working on in the special fraud unit?"

"No, I didn't even know he was an FBI agent until recently."

"Well, this is a cool man cave you got here." Michael looked around again.

"Thanks, I don't mean to be rude but my wife could be back any minute and like you said, I'm not really supposed to be here. She hates my man cave."

"Oh right, well, if I have anymore questions."

"Sure." Tim stood up and led Michael back up the stairs.

At the front door Michael said, "We'll be in touch then."

"Sure." Tim said and closed the door behind Michael.

Sally took her soup into the living room and set it on the coffee table. As she was closing up the front blinds she looked across Liberty Avenue and saw Tim pass under a streetlight. But Tim wasn't due back until tomorrow, she had heard Annie say. She watched him round the corner of Saint Charles Place and get into the passenger side of a late model Oldsmobile Cutlass. The headlights came on and the car took the turn onto Liberty. Very strange, she thought.

"I have one other thing to show you," Tim said. "Take a left down on Warner and a right again onto the old base."

"What is it?"

"It's a van. I've tricked it out with tracking, gps, and eavesdropping equipment. I call it *The Big Ear*. The software can piggyback on any network near it without being detected."

Michael was suddenly overwhelmingly lost again. "Why would you do that?"

"Why would you come into my home and start asking such obvious questions. I work for *Spectorgies*. Did it not occur to you they *might* be watching me? I am an informant for the NSA – what were you thinking?"

"The NSA? I thought it was the CIA."

"NO." Tim put his hand to his forehead. "Is there anyway I can talk to a supervisor?"

Michael pulled the car over to the side of the road. "Dude. We don't have customer service representatives. I can assure you, wholeheartedly, I don't want to be here either. I'm just an IT guy. But the fact is, you and I got put on this path together and we're going to need each other to get off it. Right? So instead of belly-aching that you've been stuck with a know nothing newbie, why don't you fill me in on what you know up to now and we'll figure out where to go from here."

Michael pulled the back onto the road and drove slowly. "Now where?"

"Take a left and go past those storage things and make a left into that trailer lot."

They got out next to a new white Sprinter van with a high roof. Tim slid the side door open and they got in. It smelled like fresh welding, Michael thought. Tim clicked on an interior light.

Michael was taken aback by the full brunt of what he was looking at. He took a seat on one of the stools as Tim flipped a couple of switches. Whirring sounds dampened the metallic echo. "Very professional."

"Thanks," Tim smiled.

193

"Did you do this yourself?"

"No. My dad was a cop in San Jose. I still have some contacts there. Well, let's just call them contacts, but I think they can be called ex-cons too." Tim said. "I made some sketches and talked them through what I needed and, *viola*. That's why I have that workshop in the basement. I did do some of the device work."

"What'd you tell them? I mean, did the ex-cons ask what this was all for?"

"Sure. I told them the truth."

"What'd they say?"

"They patted me on the shoulder and said my dad would be proud. Then I paid them *a lot* of money and said 'Don't worry about an invoice'."

Michael laughed. "Good job."

"Check this out." Tim flicked another switch and a low bass hum started. He changed the dial and the frequency of the bass went up and down. "Sound proof, like the cone of silence. Remember that?"

Michael smiled at the reference to the old "Get Smart" television show. Tim flipped the switch back off.

"This is great but what is it all for?" Michael asked.

"Transporting. General ne'er-do-well activities Rudolph had planned – his fraud cover ops and some for the actual missions. He said the future was here and he wanted to be ready."

"You know about that?"

"Sure. Rudy—"

Michael cut him off. "His name was Crane."

"Well, then, Crane. He was worried that his guy Elliot was getting too old and worried that he'd be left out here on his own. Getting you on board was taking too much time and he didn't know much about digital technology. He asked me to help him out."

"Why did he trust you so much?"

"I don't think he did. But we had a mutual friend, someone I think we both trusted."

"Who?"

"Tessa Tollison."

Michael looked up and tapped his head with his index finger. "Ah! I get it now. I see. *That's* the link."

"Right. I was worried that when Spectorgies bought out my company, Colby, I was going to get fired. See I had reached out to Tessa because she's the sister of a friend of my wife's."

"Lorna." Michael nodded.

"Yes."

And according to Ru-" Tim corrected himself, "Crane, she made calls to the NSA. Because the NSA has so many contracts within Spectorgies, they passed me through their screening process, like that." Tim snapped his fingers. "But Crane, he helped me out a lot. He showed me how that whole network operated. I mean if you're just a regular Joe working in human resources there is no way to connect the dots. Ya'know how they have one company build this part and tell them it's for a GPS guidance. Then they hire this company for another part. Then they take those products to their own company and put them together."

"Yeah, when they could just hire a couple of ex-cons and make this." Michael held out his hands and looked around.

"That's right! But then they sell the final product to the army or NSA or whoever but they don't really know what Spectorgies knows. It's a bit alarming."

"So the NSA just *expected* you to be an informant for them in return?"

"Well, it wasn't exactly that obvious. They didn't call me to the Principal's office and ask me to snitch. But one of the guys from the NSA was friendly and I guess Crane had been targeting him for a while. Anyway, Crane approached me and he really had to explain things to me. I had no idea about what was happening. I really liked Crane. He was a weird dude, but generous, ya' know?"

"Crane explained my job to me by telling me about the chalk they'd put in Nazi inkwells? Did he tell you that story?"

"Yeah, he told me."

"Looking back, I wish I had more time with the old guy." Michael said.

"I'd love to get my hands on the guy who did it. How long did you train with him?" Tim asked.

"One night."

"Wait, you only had one night with him?" Tim was astonished.

"Yeah, I was on the boat when it blew up." Michael lifted up his pant leg and pulled up the wound dressing. Blood had trickled down his leg to his sock and had crusted over the busted stitch.

"Ew!" Tim said. "And you're back here already?"

"Yeah," Michael said. "That's why I didn't know anything, well except some recent events. Crane didn't have time to do his report to Elliot."

"How did you survive that? I mean, I'm glad, but that thing took out two boats."

"I know. I was just very lucky. I haven't really processed it, I guess."

"What's Elliot like?" Tim asked.

"Old. Like *really* old. Dusty. But don't count out getting a hold of the guy who did it. We think we've got a name at least."

Tim started flipping off switches. "Oh. Yeah. Look," Tim pulled up a false panel from the desk and pulled out a small metal safe. He unlatched it and showed Michael the contents. There was a notebook wrapped in a gallon-sized plastic baggy. "This has my will, the bank accounts, everything my wife will need — should anything happen to me will you see that she gets it? I wrote it all in code, but it's easy enough that she'll understand all of it."

"Yeah man, sure." Michael nodded and watched Tim place the contents back into the false panel.

"Do you have somewhere to stay tonight?" Tim asked.

"I'll get a hotel room," Michael said. "I've got to get all that squared away."

"How 'bout this. We can go back to my hotel room. I've got a standing phone date with my wife around 9:00 and you can go get us something to eat, then we'll go over all of this and get caught up."

Michael nodded. "That would be great. Thank you."

"That way tomorrow you can start fresh and get yourself set up and we can act like we've never met." Tim said.

"Exactly how one night stands should be," Michael agreed.

Tim cut his eyes at Michael.

"Just kidding."

"But Lorna doesn't know anything about Sally's parents being CIA or any of it?" Michael said incredulously.

Tim shook his head and finished chewing. "She thinks they're dead, like everyone else. And I've seen that woman, the Nurse, over at Spectorgies a couple of times too. She was in the room when I gave a human resource meeting."

"The Nurse was Sally's boss at CIA?"

"No, no. She was a trainee with Sally in Bosnia. But the NSA snatched her up a couple of years ago."

"Well you know, they think the guy who blew up the boat was ex-CIA. A guy named Pearce."

"Why don't they pick him up?"

Michael held in a burp and puffed his chest. "Very elusive. They think he's in Portugal or some shit. Plus we don't do revenge killings."

Tim finished his soda, wiped his mouth, folded the napkin and tossed it in the food bag.

Michael stood up, picking up his mess, and pulled out his wallet. "I'm going to throw these away downstairs and get another soda. Do you want one?"

"Do you want to go get beers?"

"No, just some caffeine."

Tim nodded, "On duty."

"No, Asian. We're allergic to your guailo firewater."

"Oh yeah, I'll have one. Thanks. Here, take mine too." He handed Michael the food bag.

Tim stared at the disengaged cell phone batteries on the dresser, fighting the urge to go through Michael's carry-on bag while Michael was gone. Was he telling Michael too much? Crane had told Tim about why the FBI was keeping an eye on the NSA/Spectorgies contracts but that didn't explain why Crane was so interested in a cloaking device. Did Michael know about that?

Michael came in with two bottles of soda and tossed one to Tim. "Mind if I flop while we talk? This leg is throbbing."

"No, go ahead."

Michael plopped himself on the bed and swung his legs up.

"So," Michael started and opened his bottle of soda. "Here's what I know so far. Spectorgies was developing some type of cloaking software or a device that was to be used for the NSA."

"That's it?"

"Almost. I know the Hayward Company was involved and I know the CIA and the NRO was trying to horn in on it. Which tells us that it must have been cloaking for satellites. So the question comes in, why was Crane so interested in this operation?"

Tim felt somewhat deflated. "I was hoping you could tell me."

"After talking to Elliot and how many operations he's following, I can tell you that hearing there are other players involved – the Russians or China maybe. If Spectorgies is developing cloaking for satellites then it could also be the most powerful tool used in intelligence or counter intelligence and corporate espionage. What's to stop Spectorgies from selling it to the highest bidders?"

Tim nodded and threw his legs up into the empty chair across the table. "Maybe he was stalling them. Giving the NRO time to develop counter surveillance for the cloaking. I can only imagine everyone would want access to it. CIA, FBI, NRO, NGA, J-39..."

"Yeah, that could be." Michael scratched his head forgetting his head stitches there and winced.

"Do you have any contacts with the CIA?" Tim asked.

"No."

"Because if the CIA got wind of the Spectorgies and NSA operation through a foreign government, then it might explain that guy's presence?"

"Who? Pearce?"

"Yeah."

"Why would the CIA send someone after Crane?"

"Well, it wouldn't be hard to imagine that if the CIA found out that Crane was watching the progress, then other people would have known too – people who wanted the development and sale of the cloaking to go through."

Michael suddenly sat up and looked at Tim. "Stand up."

"Why?"

"Just do it. Stand here, next to me." Michael stood in front of the dresser mirror. Tim moved around one of the beds and stood next to him.

"Same height. Same hair-cut. We dress alike. From a distance?" Michael inspected Tim.

Tim stared at their reflections for a moment and moved back to the table and sat down. "Yeah. From a distance I think maybe someone could make that mistake."

"How close to this *are you*?" Michael asked with a new found seriousness. Had Tim been the actual target?

"It all started because I had a contact in the Hayward. He was pretty disgruntled. I was the friendly ear in human resources. He had complained about his work situation, that the software developing was sub-par and that he was putting in for a transfer for another project. I convinced him to stay and then talked to his supervisor, who was also disgruntled about the time pressure for the same project. I went back to Spectorgies in Phoenix and I got questioned about this same project. There was a lot of tension in the room and I realized that they're feeling me out. How much had these guys told me? I play innocent but tell them the truth, I tell them exactly what was said and how I felt I remedied the situation between the co-workers. So they pull me in and have me train some of the Phoenix based supervisors on this project in conflict-resolution."

"The cloaking project?"

"Yeah. I've won the trust of these guys in Spectorgies. I'm like the human resource social worker for a bunch of egomaniacs. If that bomb was meant for me *and* Crane or if they *even* knew about him, I could never have gotten this close."

"But what about the NSA and your handler with them? Could they have known?"

"I only tell them about the ego problems."

Michael clicked his tongue and shook his head. "It's more likely that someone else knows, someone with a big stake in the development. Or it could have been someone who hired Pearce from an old operation. Revenge."

"You know Keeling, a detective here on Ohlone?"

"Oh sure. I know Keeling."

"He was an informant for Crane too."

"I don't doubt that one bit," Tim said smiling. "But he's a good guy."

"After the bomb went off, I swam across the estuary here to Ohlone and Keeling pulled me out."

"Really? Well, my wife knows him better than I do." Tim did not seem at all concerned.

Michael wondered about this. "Well, he knows you are an informant."

"Really? I've always thought as far as he knows, I'm just a human resource guy. He's never given me any indication that he even knew Crane."

"So you don't think it was strange that he just so happened to be there on the bank when I washed up?"

"No. Keeling is a straight arrow. Obviously he can be trusted with a secret too. He ties his shoes in a procedural manner, ya' know the type?" But Michael had sown a seed of doubt in Tim.

"Okay."

Tim took the last swig of his soda. "As a matter of fact, there's been this thing happening with Dragon Logistics on the island. You know about that?"

"Oh, the mercenaries. They've been angling for the air space around northern California. It won't happen, too many hippies," Michael said.

"So what's next?" Tim asked. "Do I have another objective or just play it by ear. I mean, what's the goal? Getting some evidence?"

Michael rubbed his hands over his face. "How close are they in the development?"

"They're right at the end I think. Doing testing. Tweaking."

"So if they're going to make a move it will be soon?"

"You mean a sale? Yes. I was supposed to do a training meeting in the lab and it got canceled and they sent me home. On the way out I saw a lot of navy blue suits coming in."

"NSA?"

"Yeah, could've been."

"White guys?"

"Mainly."

"Did you reschedule the training?"

"Yes, it's in two weeks."

"There's no reason for you to go back?"

"No, next stop is the Hayward and then they're sending me out to some other company."

"Where?"

"I don't know - some aerospace company in L.A."

Michael leaned up from the bed and held his palms out. "Like a place that has the ability to recreate atmospheric changes?"

"Of course!" Tim smacked his forehead.

"Look, Elliot was firm about staying on this project. This is way outside my objectives. They had no idea how far along this project is. I need to make contact again."

"What were your objectives?"

"To find out what the hell was going on."

"Well, now you have so, yeah."

"You think that old beater out there will make it to Phoenix?" Michael asked.

"Yeah, what are you thinking?"

"Elliot thinks you're in Phoenix. He thinks I'm in Phoenix and I have a better chance of making contact with him and getting a response from there."

"How do you make contact?"

"Man, you've been really good to me, but I can't tell you that."

"No problem. Ancient Chinese secret. I get it."

Michael laughed. "Then I'd just sprinkle MSG on my head and click my heels together. No, this shit is a big damn production, Moscow rules, the whole nine yards."

"What do I do in the meantime?"

"Just stay close, stay trustworthy to them. I wouldn't do anything out of the norm. Business as usual."

"Right."

"I'll contact you as soon as I get word. But if you find anything out, anything big then break into someone's house, off the island, and call this secure line."

Michael wrote the phone number on a pad of paper and handed it to Tim. "Try to memorize it," he said. Then he took the second sheet off the pad and ripped it off and stuck it in his mouth and chewed for a little bit before going into the bathroom and flushing the toilet. Michael came back out and lay back down on the bed.

Tim stared at the paper, took the pencil and copied the corresponding letters down, making an alphabetical acronym out of the numbers. He crumpled it up, stuck it in his mouth, and repeated Michael's movements. Then he came back and sat down.

"Oh," Michael added. "If you ever need a safe house here, there's an apartment above a bar called the Lemon Suds. Apparently Crane used it a lot, I was told it was available." Michael suddenly felt so tired he could barely lift his head. He had a long drive tomorrow.

"I'll remember that. And look, my wife –" Tim paused. Suddenly he knew why the FBI chose Michael over him.

Michael finished the sentence for him. "Annie Doughall, nee Grey. Screaming liberal; father was a

Captain in the Air Force and mother was an artist, works for an online marketing firm."

"Yeah. Look, she knows nothing about this. Nothing. She'd divorce me if she knew.

Michael turned off his bedside lamp. "Well, then, you'd better keep her as far away from it as you can. You've done well so far. Right?"

"Yeah, just, it's been hard, the lying. She doesn't deserve – "

Michael let out a deep snore.

The next morning, Michael got up and took a shower. When he got out, Tim was sitting on the bed in his underwear with a cup of coffee, mindlessly channel surfing.

"Hey man. Where'd you get the coffee?"

Tim leaned his head over and Michael saw the small coffee pot on the dresser.

Michael turned over one of the mugs on the tray and emptied the coffee pot into it. "I wanted to thank you. I don't know where I'd be right now without your help."

Tim blinked, still sleepy. "Yeah. You're welcome."

"Crane must have been compensating you, right?"

Tim nodded and scratched himself. "Yeah, you know, he took care of me. He paid for the van too."

"Well look, make sure I fall in line with that because I don't know, ya' know, I'm still pretty new at taking his place."

Tim nodded. "We're square now, but I'll let you know."

Michael grabbed his small suitcase and headed for the door. "Take care man."

"Yeah, I'll be seeing you." Tim continued clicking through the channels.

CHAPTER 12

DRAGONS VS. DERTBAGS

What remained of the early morning fog billowed about, encircling the buildings in wispy gusts. The Ohlone DERT volunteers and firemen worked together in communal fashion preparing for the monthly graduation drill. New graduates - old, young, abled, and disabled - were joining their ranks to share the responsibility to aid themselves, their neighbors, and the emergency services in times of crisis.

Inside the drill hangar, the interior had been partitioned off with large drapes and staged into a three-story apartment building. Outside, the staging area perimeter was marked off with a row of fire engines, pylons, and a small row of trees on a grassy area. In the far corner of the parking lot, away from DERT training hangar, a large canopy had been erected. Volunteers with yellow DERT vests and backpacks milled about sleepily, finding their way back and forth to the canopy where tables had been set up and Captain Pullam's mother manned the coffee urns and boxes of donuts and bagels.

Two police cruisers sat in the parking lot away from the staging area. Commander Bill White craned his neck down and looked into a police cruiser as he walked toward the staging area. Chief Jules stood out of the way, near the row of trees watching the set up as Bill approached. He held out a large hand to Bill.

"It's good to see you again, Bill," Jules said.

Commander Bill shook Jules' hand. "Thanks for the invitation. All my men made it in time to join your DERT bags?"

Jules looked over to the volunteers clad in their yellow backpacks with the word DERT across the back and bared his teeth at Bill. "How about a cup of coffee? We got some coffee and donuts under the canopy."

"Thanks, maybe later." Bill looked around at the set up. "So, you guys go all out. You've got forty or fifty people out here. You do this every month?"

"Oh yeah. Captain Pullam said from the beginning that drilling the volunteers was essential for the response training. He's turning over a well-trained group to you. We've got 25 more graduates this month from three different sections of the island."

"What have you got inside the hangar?"

"We use a lot of the same Halloween equipment that they use for the haunted house and some of the fire department's mobile training stairs."

Bill nodded and watched some volunteers munching donuts under the canopy.

Rose and Running Bear Featherstone ate the donuts offered to them and gulped the coffee. They were both dressed uncharacteristically in matching blue mechanic jumpsuits, each of which bore a nametag patch with grey lettering that read "Martin".

"You'd think they'd offer tea as well," Rose grumbled. "Or some juice."

"Here, have a bottle of water. Take a couple of them," Running Bear offered.

Craig and Ryan came under the canopy and greeted the Featherstones.

"Huge turn-out, huh?" Craig said.

"Anything left?" Ryan asked indicating the refreshments.

"Sure, plenty for everyone," Running Bear said.

From the backseat of Annie's car, Mrs. Strangler winced as she watched Christopher and another little boy playing a game of shooting each other with their fingers and falling straight back, spread-eagle, onto the pavement. "Thank you for driving, Annie," Mrs. Strangler said getting out.

"My pleasure."

Lorna held out her right hand for Mrs. Strangler to pull herself up. "I really hope no one gets hurt today," Mrs. Strangler said, looking around at all the people with the DERT backpacks.

This struck Lorna as quite funny. "I hope no one gets hurt and has to rely on either one of us! We're like Gimpy and the Turtle to the rescue."

Mrs. Strangler chuckled as she straightened her jacket out. "Speak for yourself."

Annie stopped dead in her tracks as she watched Carol get out of her driver's seat, walk around and open the back seat of her car where Judy sat unmoving. Carol stood with her hand on her hip, saying something to the unmoving Judy.

Lorna and Mrs. Strangler looked over to the scene. "Should we?" Lorna started.

Mrs. Strangler held up her hand to stop Lorna. "No. That's family business over there."

Charley and Wyatt sat in the Jeep and watching Chief Jules and Bill chatting. "What do you think we should do?" asked Charley.

Wyatt shook his head. "Just do what we've been doing, I guess."

"But what if Bill outs us to the Chief? Forget the DERT program - they'll run us out of town. I'll lose my new job."

"Charley, you haven't even been hired yet," Wyatt said, perturbed. He threw open his car door. "Come on! Whatever we have waiting for us, can't be as bad as sitting here waiting for it."

Keeling walked into his office, picked up the phone receiver, and pushed a blinking button on the phone. "Keeling."

"Yeah, this is Jeffers from Ohlone Sun Times."

Keeling knew the news editor on a first name basis. The fact that Jerry Jeffers skipped the niceties made Keeling's skin crawl. Keeling braced himself.

"Look, Keeling, this is a courtesy call. I'm hoping you can either confirm or hopefully deny this report for me."

"Okay."

Jeffers cleared his throat. "Is Ohlone PD investigating one of their own in the death of Jimmy Marsh?"

Keeling looked through his glass partition across into his Captain's empty office. "I'm going to need more, Jerry. You know, I couldn't comment on such a thing. That's for internal affairs."

"Apparently there were eyewitness accounts of the Ohlone Police dumping something from the back of a cruiser into the estuary. Goes on to say, calls to your department about the sightings have been ignored and the Ohlone PD is working to cover it up before it gets to internal affairs."

"Cover what up?" Keeling realized his slip and added quickly, "Jeffers, there is no cover up. We're currently working all angles in the death of Jimmy Marsh. Look,

I'm not going to make a statement about an ongoing investigation." Keeling slammed down the receiver and dialed a number.

"Internal Affairs, Crawley," the voice said.

"It's Keeling at Ohlone. Can you get over here today?"

"Sure, what's up?"

"We've got a cover up about to explode on the front page."

"Whoa, okay. About an hour?" Crawley asked.

"As soon as you can," Keeling said and hung the phone up. He took a deep breath and dialed another number.

"Hello?"

"Captain, I'm sorry to bother you at home," Keeling explained.

"What it is?" the Captain asked.

"We've got a problem. I'm afraid it's an internal one and it's going to hit the Sunday papers."

"Shit. I'm on my way." The Captain hung up.

Keeling pushed another button on his phone.

"Desk."

"It's Keeling. I'm going to need the vehicle assignments for the last week. Also, please get someone from CSI to the motor pool. I'll meet them there."

Captain Pullam had partnered up the graduating classes and split them into three teams of eight. Due to the odd number of graduates, Roberta graciously volunteered to even up the teams. Annie and Judy, Carol and Roberta, with four members of Section 6 made up Team A and would be on incident command first. Lorna and Mrs. Strangler, Wyatt and Charley with two members of Section 6 and two from Section 11 made up Team B. Team B would start in triage. Rose and Running Bear, Ryan and Craig, Christopher and John with the two graduates of section 11 made up Team C and they would start in search and rescue.

Pullam addressed the volunteers from the back of pickup truck. "Inside the hangar are 18 bodies, and all have varying degrees of injuries or death. Search and rescue, you'll retrieve these bodies. Triage, you'll tend to them. And Incident Command, you're in charge of communications, haz-mat, supplies, and maintaining some semblance of order. There will be three drills. Teams will rotate into the responsibilities. I will mark the beginning and end of each drill with this horn. Ready?" Pullam lifted the horn.

"Wait!" Craig stopped Pullam. "Is that it? I mean don't we have a map of the building or anything?"

"Nope."

"Come on! You've got to get us something to go on," Ryan reiterated Craig's response.

"Okay, it was a 7.6 earthquake. And don't ask the men inside the building for help either. They are there to observe and make sure no one gets hurt." Pullam struck an uncharacteristic harsh tone. "This isn't Rock and Roll fantasy camp! You are trained first responders! Organize yourselves!" Pullam raised the horn and yelled, "Go!"

Everyone quickly picked their backpacks up from the ground and scrambled around into their groups. Luckily for Team B, they had Charley, who had set up their triage unit and organized their medical sections and morgue within the first five minutes. Team A was having issues deciding who would be their incident commander and, incidentally, where to set up their incident command post. As Team C donned their rescue gear, Ryan looked up at the hangar and watched the white smoke seep out the top window.

"What's with the smoke?" Ryan asked pulling on his hard hat.

Running Bear looked up to the window. "It's a fog machine. It's just water vapors. But if there is old oil and grease on the floor, it might make it a little slippery."

Ryan nodded.

Mrs. Jules sat in the busy Trident diner finishing her ham and eggs. Mayor Williams walked in and began shaking hands with the diners.

Glynnis looked up from her plate, saw Mayor Williams and grinned. "Oh, this is going to be good."

Lorna sat on the tarp laid out for the walking wounded. She watched as Team C went into the hangar and took in the rest of the scene around her. Over at Incident Command, Annie was being shadowed by zombie Judy. What kind of illness could a brain have that it has to be so heavily doped into submission?

Wyatt peered out from the line of trees where the temporary "morgue" had been set up and motioned at Lorna. Lorna got up to join him.

"Look, I need to talk to you about Jimmy and that fall you took," he said. "When you fell into that pit and landed on Jimmy, did you find or see, like, a folder? Was he holding anything? Did he have a back pack or something?"

"I don't know. I mean, it was really dark – how do you know about that?"

"I was just wondering. I think the Featherstones had something to do with it," Wyatt continued.

"Me too! Why do you think it's the Featherstones?"

"Okay but I have to trust you will hear me out before you react."

"Have we been married?"

"Just promise."

"Sure.

Wyatt took a deep breath and lowered his head. "Charley and I work for Dragon."

Lorna's eyes grew into enormous blue orbs. She growled quietly through mashed teeth, "WHAT?"

"We didn't fit in. So Commander Bill, the little guy in blue over there, sent us to *infiltrate* the DERT program. We didn't know all of this was going to go down and now Wild Bill thinks *you* have the file. Look it's not important right now."

"It is to me!" Lorna said.

"Please just listen. There was this file folder that Bill never let out of his sight, right? Well, accidentally, I got a look at it one time. I thought it was the originals for another file I was making copies of and by the time I figured out it wasn't what I thought it was, Bill came in and said that the file was for his eyes only. See, that's when I realized there are two sets of books. One is the same one we give to volunteer programs like you guys and one is the actual plans for dismantling the DERT program."

"Wyatt. Get to your point." Lorna was growing agitated with his explanation.

"Carol gave Charley a binder that she put together for her nursing home DERT program and some of it was straight out of the book I had accidentally seen in Bill's file folder."

"So?"

"How did Carol get a hold of it?"

You did it, she wanted to say. Only you knew about both the drill and the file. You're the link. Now you're panicked and pointing fingers at everyone else to divert suspicion from yourself. But instead she said, "Who else knew about that drill? Who knew about that file? How would Jimmy know which file to take?"

Wyatt looked completely defeated. "Jimmy came to warn me. He said the FBI was on to Dragon. He said he was being sent on a mission to retrieve documentation that they were committing fraud. I felt sorry for him, y' know? I thought he was full of shit. Then he started talking about how he knew we were doing the drill, and he knew about the evacuation and the plans for reconstructing the military base for Dragon's security forces. That's what I saw in Bill's files. So, I told him what the file looked like. I just didn't know what else to do."

"So the Featherstones told him about the drill and sent Jimmy down to steal the file. He steals the file and Bill kills him? Are the Featherstones with the FBI?"

"No. If Bill had killed Jimmy, then Carol wouldn't have those pages. You see? There had to be a third party. And no one else knew about Jimmy going down there except the Featherstones, well, and me."

"Yeah," Lorna said with finality and walked over to Mrs. Strangler who was helping Charley tend to a "victim." She looked around the staging area that was consumed in the drill activity. Incident Command had people urgently talking on walkie-talkies and milling about with papers and maps. She mindlessly wrapped a gauze bandage around a "walking wounded" victim's head. So we've been asking the wrong questions, she thought. It's not who knew Jimmy was there - it's who knew the Dragon drill was happening there.

"I'm not a Sikh," the volunteer victim said.

"What?" Lorna looked down at the victim.

"It's enough gauze."

"Oh right." Lorna tore off the end and tucked it into the victim's gauze turban.

Running Bear was dragging a headless dummy from the hangar to the triage area. Rose was running behind him with the head.

"That fog machine is making it too slippery to work in there!" Running Bear was yelling at one of the firemen.

John stood at the hangar door holding it open and letting the fog-smoke billow out as Christopher dutifully helped a "walking wounded" over to triage. Wyatt came back over to the tarps as the next wave of victims arrived and stood next to Lorna.

"I just don't see Rose and Running Bear as the FBI type, Wyatt."

"I know. I don't know what else—every time I try to help something bad happens."

Lorna looked up into his pale face. "Let's get through the drill first."

Mrs. Strangler came up. "You've got bodies to move into the morgue, mister."

"Yes ma'am," Wyatt said.

Lorna looked over to the Incident Command Post. She really needed to talk to Annie. But it seemed that there were so many people wandering about now, making it impossible for her to find Annie. Lorna walked back over to the "walking wounded" tarp to see Judy standing there staring at her. Lorna looked down. Annie was lying on the tarp at Judy's feet.

"What are you doing?" Lorna said.

Annie didn't move.

Lorna knelt down over Annie. "Hey. What are you doing?"

Annie opened one eye. "Trade bags with me."

"I have to talk to you. I think..." Lorna stopped and looked up at Judy.

Annie muttered urgently, "Just trade bags! Do it casually."

"Okay." Lorna stood up and put her bag down next to Annie and said loudly, "You're fine now – go back to work."

Annie got up and grabbed Lorna's backpack. "Come on Judy."

Lorna watched them walk back to Incident Command relatively unnoticed. It seemed like the number of people was growing - there had to be at least a hundred people out here now.

As the drill horn sounded, indicating the end of the first drill, Lorna pulled Mrs. Strangler aside. "I have to run to the bathroom real quick."

"Well hurry! We're on search and rescue and we have to—" Mrs. Strangler was saying.

Lorna ran into the porta-potty and ripped open the backpack. Holy crap! Now she *really did* have the missing file. She zipped the bag back up and ran over to her group as they finished cleaning up the triage area.

Wyatt grabbed Lorna by her cast. "Listen, when we go in there," he indicated the hangar, "stay close to me. Bill has men in there and I don't...just stay close to me."

Lorna nodded. Did he see Annie trade bags with her? She had to hide this bag. Why didn't Annie give the bag to Roberta? Where had it come from? Panic swelled in her chest. She looked around the staging area. She needed to hide.

"What's the matter with you?"

Lorna looked down at Mrs. Strangler who was poking her in the shoulder.

"Ow! Stop poking me."

"Well, get your gear on then." Mrs. Strangler was wearing her helmet, a couture scarf for a mask, and Fine Leather Gloves – a little General Patton in drag.

Lorna pulled off her bag, since there was no rescue equipment in it. Where the hell was Annie? Lorna leaned down to Mrs. Strangler. "Trade bags with me."

"Are you having flashbacks?"

"What?"

"9/11. Are you having a flashback? Annie told me you were there."

"No. Just trade bags with me." Lorna turned around and made sure no one could hear her. "I have the file. The one I got arrested for?"

Mrs. Strangler glared at her. "Give it to me."

Lorna traded backpacks with Mrs. Strangler. She watched as Mrs. Strangler boldly marched over to

Captain Pullam's mother, who sat nodding off under the coffee canopy. Mrs. Strangler quietly traded backpacks and marched back over to Lorna.

"Here."

Lorna bit her lower lip. "Thanks." Lorna opened the backpack and pulled out the hard-hat, goggles, gloves, flashlight and dust mask.

"We ready?" Wyatt smiled at the group.

"Mrs. Strangler, I think it's best we let Charley and Wyatt run the search party and you and I wait out here," Lorna said.

"Hey!" Charley objected. "You two could search! You'll just have to lead out the walking wounded and Wyatt and I can do the heavy lifting."

"There you go Charley - good thinking," Mrs. Strangler encouraged him.

Lorna cut her eyes at Charley for undermining her.

Wyatt looked up at the building. A puff of smoke seeped out a window at the top.

A fireman popped out of the door wearing his fire gear. "You have a three story walk up in here. Inside you have other firefighters to help guide you. There are 12 apartments, some have tenants in them and some of the tenants are dead. Your job is to bring them all to safety."

The drill horn sounded again and they went in to the dark cavernous hangar together and stood at the bottom of a flight of stairs. Lorna could hear "victims" calling for help and footsteps pounding above her. By flashlight, the massive hangar had been transformed into a movie set of an apartment hallway masked off from the rest of the hangar by a three-story drape. And the pit she had fallen into was on the far side of the drape. She poked her head through the drape as the others began to take the stairs. She cut off her flashlight and slid behind the drape.

A hand reached out and horse-collared Lorna. A hand covered her mouth. Annie whispered frantically, "It's me," a second too late.

Lorna whipped her arm at the elbow and whacked the person with her cast.

"Ow! Mmm. Oh."

"Damn! I'm sorry! I'm sorry Annie - it's me," Lorna whispered in the dark.

"Why did you hit me?"

"I'm sorry. Sh, sh, I'm sorry. Are you okay?"

"Be more careful with that thing. Stop groping me. Mm, I think you gave me a fat lip."

"Okay, shush now," Lorna whispered. "Where did you get that backpack?"

"I don't know. I set mine down for a minute and then when I went to put my water bottle in it, I saw it wasn't mine."

The sound of boots shuffling stopped them talking. They crouched down in unison as they watched a shadow from the far side of the drape walk over to the oil-changing pit, heard a thud, and watched the shadow turn back and leave. They waited another moment as the drape stopped moving.

"How did you get rid of Judy?" Lorna whispered.

"I didn't. She's right behind me."

Lorna turned on her flashlight. Annie held up her hand to show zombie Judy attached to it.

"Oh my God, Annie."

"What'd you want me to do? It's not like she's going to *tell* anyone."

"Okay, well look. I'm going over to the pit. You two stay here and be my lookout."

Lorna took a couple of steps toward the oil-changing pit and slid a little, almost losing her balance. She shuffled as quietly as she could the rest of the way and lowered herself down into the pit. She clicked on her flashlight. She saw a small cement stairway on the far side and shook her head. Well, that would have been useful to know, she thought. She grabbed the backpack that had been dropped into the pit and unzipped it. Bundles of cash fell out. She quickly replaced them and zipped it back up.

"What'd you find?" Annie whispered when she got back.

"It's cash."

"Cash, money?"

"Yes, so this has to be, like, a drop, right?"

"So someone has to come pick it up."

"Right. But Annie, you can't be here with your friend."

"Then they'll look for an exchange, right?"

"Maybe they already think they got the exchange. Somebody must have changed bags with you by mistake. All the DERT bags look alike."

Annie burst into a giggle. "I'm sorry. It's the stress. You're right."

"Look, you go back and I'll wait here."

"No, no - we should get Roberta."

"If she comes back in here, then it'll be obvious. We can't risk it."

"But how will I know if you need help? What if they come back?"

"Look - I won't go near it. If I see someone, I'll just turn on my light, see who it is, and make a bee line out of here. No one would dare do anything with all those witnesses."

Annie exhaled. "Okay, you're right. Someone will come looking for that bag."

"Oh, but listen. Wyatt admitted to me that he was working for Dragon. I don't know quite how but I think he is neck deep in this whole thing, and I think he's been trying to throw shade on everyone else."

"What?"

"I know. I was shocked too."

"I don't know what you mean by throw shade."

"He's been trying to divert suspicion on himself, and maybe Charley."

"Okay I'll keep an eye on him. Please Lorna, be careful. Just see who it is and leave. Agreed?"

"Yes."

Annie's flashlight pointed to the floor. "Come on Judy."

Outside the hangar door, Annie ran smack into Mrs. Strangler. "What's going on with you two?" Mrs. Strangler wanted to know.

"Nothing," Annie said in the high-pitched guilt of a student passing a note.

"Where's Lorna?"

"Um."

Mrs. Strangler bore a hole with her eyes through Annie.

Annie looked over to the hangar.

"Okay." Mrs. Strangler nodded her head in understanding and gave Judy the once over before walking away.

Annie looked around for Carol as the drill horn sounded.

Roberta walked over. "Where've you been? Carol was looking for you."

"I just took Judy for a walk."

Roberta squinted down at Annie. "Where's Lorna?"

"I don't know. With her group?"

"Well, we have to do search and rescue next. You better put your gear on."

Annie held up her hand that was attached to Judy.

"Oh. Well, uh, I don't know. I guess you and Carol can trade off."

"That would be fine," Annie agreed.

The Disaster Relief Club

The final drill horn sounded. Mrs. Strangler was very happy to have a seat at the Incident Command Post as two members of the Section 6 team took charge. She looked over to Mrs. Pullam who was setting out the lunch boxes on the tables under the canopy. The yellow DERT bag sat untouched, leaning against the chair.

Lorna waited against the drape shifting her weight. She heard the drill horn sound, but still no movement. It was completely possible that Wyatt had pushed Jimmy into the pit and had been blackmailing Dragon. He could have learned about Carol's plans for the nursing homes and gave her part of the folder – just to implicate her. But then how did Annie get the backpack if Wyatt had been with her over in triage.

Lorna heard the hangar door open, the "victims" began their wailing, and footsteps start up the stairs. What if someone was above her, watching her watch the pit, waiting for her to leave?

Rose and Ron finished setting up the triage area with blankets and tarps. John Wu pulled out a small first aid kit. To John Wu's embarrassment, Rose pulled out a box of women's sanitary pads and a bottle of vinegar from her backpack.

"What are you doing?" John asked her, pointedly referring to the box of pads and shielding Christopher's view.

Running Bear stood up to John. "If someone is bleeding to death they aren't going to need your *band-aids*, man. Do you have hospital grade bandages and sterile wash so you can wash out the wounds? Will you have access to medical supplies? No."

"This was all in our binder John, under the triage section," Rose added, continuing to unwrap the sanitary pads.

Wyatt sat down next to Mrs. Strangler. "I'm glad we've got a minute here, Mrs. Strangler."

Mrs. Strangler turned to Wyatt.

"I know something about the night Jimmy died, and I've been afraid." Wyatt looked out into the distance and choked on his words.

Annie and Judy wandered over to them. Wyatt looked at the ground.

"Yes?" Mrs. Strangler asked Annie.

Annie stared at Wyatt for a beat. "Oh, we were just –" Annie realized she needed to walk away and turned back around to find Captain Pullam standing in front of her.

"What are you doing? You're supposed to be in search and rescue," he said to Annie.

Annie looked up at the Captain questioningly and held out her hand that Judy was attached to.

Pullam said, "Judy? I'd trust her with this drill before anyone else."

"Why?"

"You know that little tumbler we had this weekend? Judy beat me to the DERT facility. I roll up about 5:30 and there she is standing at the facility door. Not bad for a schizophrenic."

Wyatt perked up. "Wait a second now. Judy was *here* at 5:30 the morning of the earthquake. Was she carrying anything?"

"Sure she had a bag with her. I saw her standing next to the building and said 'Good job Judy. Do you want to go home now? Your mom is missing you.' And she got in the truck and I took her back to Portside," Pullam said smiling at Annie expectantly.

Lorna saw a beam of light shoot across the floor of the hangar. She watched as someone carefully made their way across the wall on the far side of the hangar. A tiny beam of light moved into the middle of the hangar just above the pit. Lorna watched as the beam of light disappeared down the pit stairs.

From the far corner she heard a man's voice. "It's go time, Austin. Hit it!"

Lorna watched another shadow move fast toward the pit. She flipped on her flashlight and trained it on the moving body. But he was moving so fast like he was floating. Lorna took several long quick strides forward trying to get a look at who it was but slid forward, backpedaled, and fell forward. The further she slid, the faster she careened toward the pit.

"FIRE! FIRE! FIRE!"

All eyes cut toward the hangar. Volunteers and firemen streamed out of the hangar door hacking and coughing.

Annie grabbed Wyatt. "Lorna's in there."

People were running out of the building as fast as people were running to the building. Mrs. Strangler calmly got up and walked over to the canopy and grabbed the DERT backpack with the files in it and put it on.

Lorna slammed into the body standing on the edge of the pit, sending the body violently down. With her flashlight still on, she looked down into the pit and saw Carol crouched down in the corner, holding the money backpack. The body of a young man lay curled up against the wall unconscious. Carol was looking not at Lorna, but above her. Lorna could hear someone yelling from behind. Looking back, Lorna saw the drape had caught fire and was burning fast.

"Carol, help me get him out of here."

Carol put the backpack, "Okay."

Lorna carefully made her way down the steps and checked his pulse. When she looked back, Carol had made her way up the stairs and was walking away.

Lorna screamed, "HEY!!! HELP! WE'RE IN THE PIT!" She struggled to turn the man's body around. "Come on! WAKE UP!"

She looked up and saw the entire drape and part of the wall had burst into flame. She continued screaming and struggled to drag the man by his collar toward the stairs. She pulled the body up on one step and grabbed him around the chest. Pushing up with her legs, she heaved him up another step. If she could get him out of the pit she could slide him out the rest of the way on that cement. The smoke was burning her throat and she closed her eyes, mustering all her strength to pull him up one stair at a time.

"Lorna!"

Lorna opened her eyes to see Santa Claus towering above her. Three firemen jumped into the pit and rolled the man off her onto a stretcher. Lorna tried to stand up but slipped. Santa's arm bolted out and caught her mid-fall and yanked her up out of the pit. She fainted.

"She what?"

Annie was laughing so hard that Tim had a hard time hearing her. Annie took a deep breath and leaned back. "She fainted."

"Well I'm glad she's okay."

"Where did they take Judy?"

"She's still in the nursing home. Hopefully, now with Carol gone, they'll recheck her dosage."

"So wait. Judy had followed Jimmy to the hangar. He fell in the pit during the quake and presumably died. Judy takes the file from him and goes to the Red Cross and DERT training facility. Why?"

"I guess she couldn't figure out where else to go."

"So, Pullam finds her and takes her home to the nursing facility. Her mother gets her hands on the file. Then after Lorna falls into the pit and discovers the body all hell broke loose, huh?"

"Yes. Apparently Carol found the evidence of the pay off to Delores Tam, and instead of taking it to the authorities – which was a good thing, because Dragon had bought off that Ohlone Fraud Division detective—"

"Jenkins?"

"Right. Instead, Carol decided to get paid off too, by blackmailing Delores. Anyway, Jenkins threw Jimmy's body into the estuary."

"That's so horrible."

"I know. And Jenkins thought Lorna had the file and went after her."

"Jenkins or Dragon?" Tim asked.

"I don't know. I guess they're working all that out now."

Tim paused. "Hang on. How did Keeling know Jenkins moved the body?"

"I don't know. I imagine someone had to see something. I'm sure Keeling has his informants and whatever."

Tim thought about what Michael had said about Keeling being on the shore when the boats blew up. "Keeling the dragon-slayer. No more Dragons on the island. I think that's good."

"Me too, I don't want our little town to become part of a military complex. It's bad enough you work for Spectorgies."

"What if we moved?"

"Where?"

"Phoenix?"

"Tim, I am *not* moving to Phoenix."

Tim chuckled. "I know. Just a thought. You wouldn't have to worry about dragons or dragon-slayers though."

Annie pinched his belly.

"Ow!" Tim cuddled his wife and kissed her deeply. "I just want to keep you safe."

EPILOGUE

Lorna and Sally walked their landlords out the front door and said goodbye to them.

Sally shut the front door and leaned against it. Lorna folded her arms, with her newly wrapped cast, across her chest and slowly shook her head.

"They didn't even offer to reduce our rent," Lorna said and walked into the living room.

"Three months without a kitchen? And have construction workers here every day? How are you supposed to work in those conditions?" Sally added.

"This isn't going to work. We've got Tessa coming and –"

Sally cut her off. "Forget Tessa. We won't have a kitchen for three months!"

Lorna plopped down on the couch.

"Maybe we can ask them to delay the construction," Lorna said.

The doorbell rang.

"Or move," Sally said before opening the front door.

Glynnis and Mrs. Jules stood holding a bouquet of flowers. "I'm sorry to just show up like this," Glynnis said.

Sally didn't know what to say.

"I'm Glynnis Jules."

"And I'm Esther Jules," the elderly woman said. "We've come by to check on Lorna."

"Please come in." Sally said. "Lorna?"

Lorna got up from the couch as the older woman entered the living room.

"Oh!" Glynnis said. "A hero and beautiful to boot!" She hugged Lorna. "My husband is very taken with your bravery."

"Yes," Esther said handing her the bouquet, "and we wanted to invite you to our golf club."

"Thank you," Lorna said.

"After your arm heals, of course," Esther added.

Lorna looked pleadingly at Sally, who was stifling a laugh. "I'm sorry, I don't play golf." Lorna started.

Glynnis clapped her hands. "Oh wonderful, Mother can teach you!"

Esther nodded proudly.

"Would you ladies like some tea?" Sally offered.

Esther answered. "No, no, don't bother. We just came by to meet this young lady and thank her. Now we must go. There is a hearing on the city council we want to attend." She looked at Lorna. "Now, you rest and we'll check back in on you in a month"

The two women showed themselves out, leaving Lorna holding the bouquet with her mouth open.

Sally closed the door behind them and collapsed on the floor laughing hysterically and gasped out, "Mother will teach you!"

ABOUT THE AUTHOR

Saylor Billings lives with her family in Northern California. She is a writer and producer for Billibatt Productions.

To listen to the O Line Mysteries free podcast go to **www.olinemysteries.com**. There you will find 48 episodes filled with mystery, friendship, and laughter.

Coming Soon from M. Saylor Billings

The Rot is Deep: Book 3 of
The O Line Mysteries Series

The O Line Mystery Short Stories

Red, White, and Scotch: Book 4 of
The O Line Mysteries Series

Writing as Lorna Tollison:
Nobody, really, Likes You
A Guide to Insouciance.

A satirical look at self help books and the world of Reality Television…by a fictional character.